The Help of Angels

THE HELP OF ANGELS

A historical novel with an unearthly twist

H.J. Zeger

Sunbridge Books
Deerfield Beach. Florida

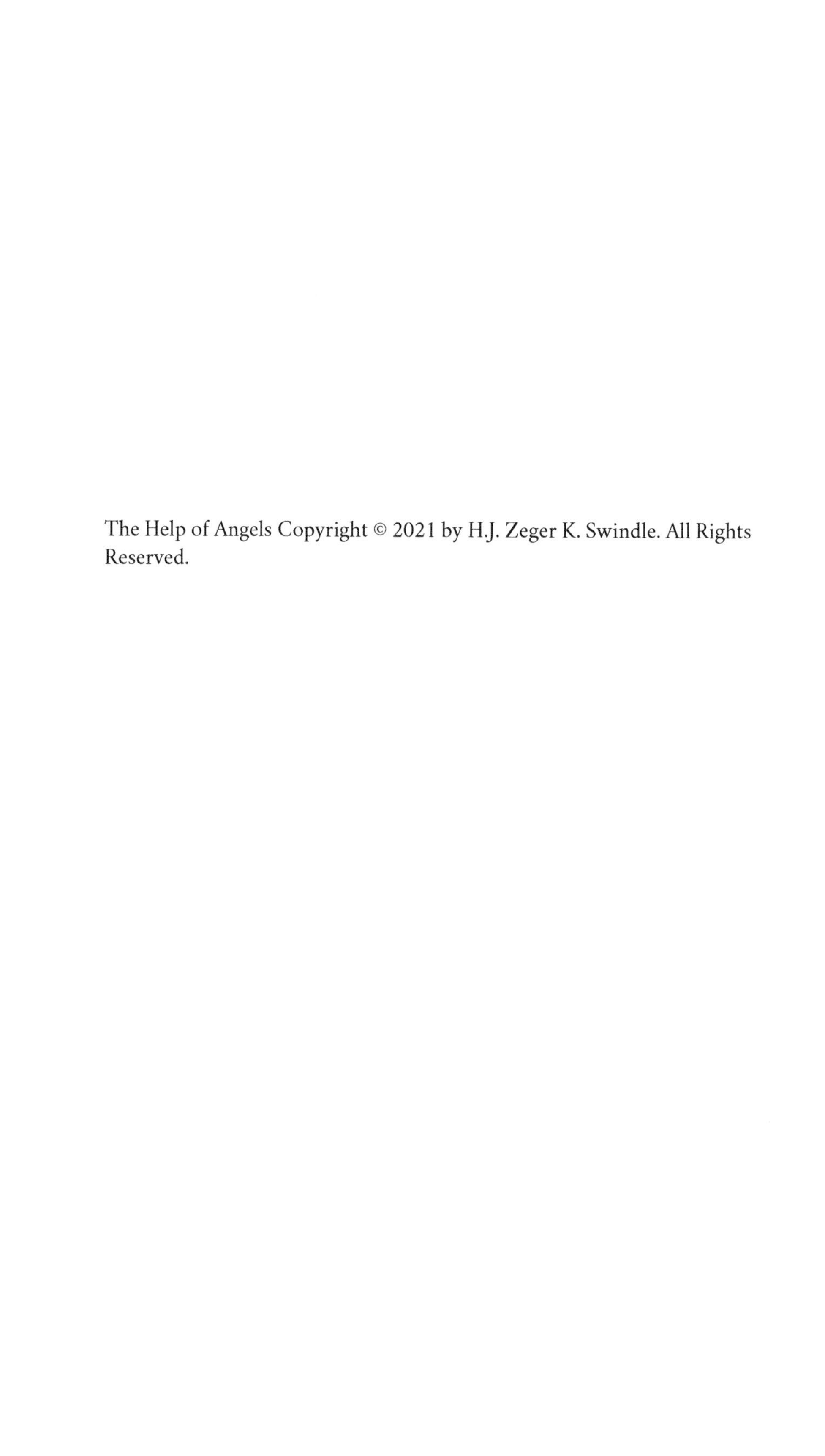

The Help of Angels

a historical novel with an unearthly twist

H.J. Zeger

Sunbridge Books
Deerfield Beach, Florida

"Suffering anywhere concerns men and women everywhere."

Elie Wiesel

Dedicated to my mother and father

Author's Note

Emil Zeger and Seren Shwartz were raised in a small city in Hungary called Beregszász, located by the foothills of the Carpathian Mountains. Today, Beregszász is a territory of the Ukraine. Emil and Seren probably didn't know each other growing up, but their paths most likely crossed at least once. During the Second World War, in their early twenties, they were placed in concentration camps. Those two people later became my mother and father.

The character Benjamin Weiss is the protagonist in The Help of Angels. He was based on my father, but unlike Benjamin who ends up being taken out of a concentration camp and placed into the safekeeping of a Benedictine monastery, my father never had that good fortune. Ben's parents, Mendel and Hanni Weiss, portray my grandparents on my father's side, Adolph and Hanni Zeger. Ben's four brothers and three sisters represent my father's siblings: Ignatz, Morris, Arnon, Herschel, Margaret, Serena and Rosie.

I never had the opportunity of meeting my father's parents and three of his four brothers, but through the writing process, we got acquainted by a kind of channeling, or psychic communication; I would visualize their bodies and faces, and listen to their voices from the great beyond. The further I searched the past—the more those relatives I never met—revealed themselves on the pages.

While I was surfing the web several years ago, by chance or otherwise, I discovered the names of my great-grandfather and great-grandmother on my father's side; Baruch and Leah Zeger. They lived during the 1800s, in or near Beregszász. I found little information regarding my great grandparents, although I can tell you the name of one their sons, Adolph, who was my father's father. He was born around 1888. Baruch and Leah raised Adolph to be a mensch (a Yiddish word defined as a man of integrity and honor). Adolph married Hanni (Chava) Rosen, and the small but strong woman eventually gave birth to three daughters and five sons, named in the previous paragraph.

Adolph Zeger earned a decent living in Beregszász by delivering packages from a horse-drawn wagon; an early Federal Express service so to speak. Hanni, Adolph, and their eight children received their milk from a cow they kept in the backyard barn. They raised their own chickens which provided them an ample supply of fresh eggs. My grandfather was not a wealthy man, yet he had the means to feed his family, buy them new clothes for the Jewish holidays, and put a roof over their heads. That all came to a crashing halt one day.

By March of 1944, disaster struck the Jews living in Beregszász, and all over Hungary: German troops invaded the country, and high booted Nazi soldiers trod up and down the main streets of Hungary's cities, shaming Jews by ordering them to sew and wear yellow Stars of David onto their outer garments. Next, the German and Hungarian armies forced Jewish residents out of their businesses and homes, transporting them to crowded, unsanitary, and inhumane detention centers, or ghettos. (The foreshadowing of the concentration camps.)

Between May and August of 1944, an alliance of German and Hungarian authorities arrested my father, his father and mother, his brother Herschel, sister Rosie, and approximately 3,600 of the remaining Jews living in Beregszász at the time, and they brought them to a brick factory on the outskirts of town. There, the displaced residents waited days or weeks for trains to deport them to various camps throughout Europe. During that time period, my father, his parents, a brother, and a sister, along with thousands of other men, women, children, and infants were crammed into boxcars. The trains left Beregszász and towns and cities all over Hungary, enroute to various camps. My father woke up at a train station in Mauthausen, Austria, where he and the large group from Hungary were marched through the town, then imprisoned at the Mauthausen concentration camp.

My father's parents, his sister Rosie, and his brother Herschel disembarked the train at the Auschwitz death camp, located in German-occupied Poland. Along with hundreds from Hungary, the four of them walked onto the train platform, where they participated in a selection process supervised by Nazi medical doctors. The deportation trains constantly delivered thousands more terrified adults, babies and children into Auschwitz day and night. Many of them had suffocated inside the boxcars before they arrived at their destination.

Adolph and Hanni Zeger were most likely murdered in the gas chambers, or by some other method, the same day they set foot in Auschwitz. Their names are recorded in the "Hall of Records" at the Yad Vashem World Holocaust Remembrance Center, in Jerusalem, Israel. There is no record of what happened to their youngest son, Herschel; he was either murdered the same day he arrived at the death camp or died from some other cause at a later date inside the camp. A young, Rosie Zeger was registered as a prisoner of Auschwitz.

Seren, my mother, was hiding in Budapest, Hungary when the Gestapo arrested her. They put her on a deportation train in Budapest, and she disembarked at Bergen Belsen, a notorious concentration camp that was once located in the northern part of Germany. An estimated 50,000 or more prisoners were exterminated there. The British and Canadian armies liberated Belsen on April 15, 1945. When the Allied forces arrived, they found approximately 60,000 starved and diseased men, women, and children. Despite the large number receiving immediate medical attention and food, many of those prisoners were in such ill health they only lived past a few days.

My mother and the other women survivors in her group hung onto life while a Swedish relief organization helped them out of Bergen Belsen; they were taken by ship to a Christian convent in Sweden, where nuns, nurses, and doctors spent weeks nursing the gaunt and sickly survivors back to health. After she left the convent, my mother briefly worked at a factory in Sweden before sailing on an ocean liner from Stockholm to America. The huge ship docked at Ellis Island, off the coast of New York City, where from 1892 to 1954, nearly 12 million new immigrants, including my mother, took their first step in becoming a legal citizen of the United States of America. My mother's Aunt Esther (her mother's sister), who once lived on the Grand Concourse in the Bronx, not far from the old Yankee stadium, had sponsored my mother to come live in America. She was taken under her aunt's wing, and she started a new life there.

After my father was liberated from Mauthausen, he returned to his hometown of Beregszász, where he found the Russian army had confiscated his father's house and property. He reunited with his only surviving brother, Morris, who had spent a length of time in a labor camp in the Russian province of Siberia. The orphaned brothers left Beregszász in the late 1940s and immigrated by jet to America. They settled in Newburgh, by their beloved sisters, Margaret, Serena, and Rosie.

In the early 1950s, a young and brave Emil and Seren, still unknown to one another were officially introduced by relatives in New York City. The man and woman from Beregszász, Hungary were married in a traditional Jewish wedding that was held in the Bronx. The couple settled in Newburgh and raised a family of two sons and one daughter.

When my Aunt Rosie came to America, she met and married Ralph Monitz. They became my godparents when I was born. In my adolescence, I had attended seventh through ninth grade at South Junior High School in Newburgh. The school is in the Heights, an area not far from where my Uncle Ralph and Aunt Rosie once lived. Sometimes during my school lunch break, I would quickly walk over and eat at their house. On one of those afternoons during lunch, my aunt and I were sitting in her kitchen, looking out onto the backyard. I glanced at the blue numbers tattooed on the inside of her forearm. I never had the courage to ask my aunt about the numbers before then; I did that day. She got mad, then extremely uncomfortable, rapidly placing a hand, or a sleeve of a sweater over the embarrassing tattoo of numerals. She awkwardly explained: "They gave me the numbers when I went inside the concentration camp." That was the first and the last time I spoke to my aunt regarding Auschwitz, or any other camp for that matter.

My parents and relatives suffered greatly because of what they went through in the Holocaust. I saw it in their eyes. The camp memories must have haunted them terribly at times, as if they wanted to wake up from a dreadful nightmare but could not. For the life of me, I will never fathom how anyone coped with that experience. My mom and dad were strong and brave. My dad used to say, "the lice in the camp ate us up alive". My father discussed his time in the camp to whomever would listen. My mother was just the opposite. I think she dealt with her phantom memories of Bergen Belsen—and what happened to her there—by storing that deep, dark past far, far away; in a place she never wanted to revisit. I sensed her sadness at times; it reflected in the pools of her dark-brown eyes. She was a beautiful woman. My father was a beautiful man.

My early exposure to the Holocaust inevitably caused me considerable sadness and depression growing up. Sometimes it still does. I was angered my parents and so many more people had to go through that hell. When I became a teenager, I wanted my mother and father to talk to someone about being in the camps and receive some sorely needed therapy. Whenever I asked her, my mother would only reply, "I don't have a problem—I don't need to talk to anyone". It was basically the same story with my father. I eventually obtained psychotherapy regarding the Holocaust story. Writing this book was an extremely deep-felt therapy.

My mother and father remained strong throughout their lives. And even though they were hardened by their experiences in the camps, they continued to be caring, hardworking, and loving human beings.

Each and every soul who comes to this planet must discover for themselves, that love and respect for nature, the planet's creatures, and our fellow brothers and sisters may be the only sane path to follow. At least the only path I want to pursue. I don't have an answer why millions of Jews and Gentiles perished in the Holocaust. And only thousands survived. I do feel that many could not go on living, given the circumstances they were faced with, and even death might have been a better choice for them than life. I feel that they, (the ones who did not survive) were helped to leave this life and continue on with their journey. I only wish God had intervened and stopped the Genocide from happening in the first place.

You may ask, where do these angels fit into the story? Who are they? What are they? Where were they during the war? Angels are spoken about in the holy Bible several times. In the New and Old Testament alike. Are they higher beings? Celestial beings. Spiritual guides. Divine helpers. Messengers. Agents of God? I can only speak for myself about this phenomenon, but I do know that I have been assisted and guided by a spiritual force along the paths that I will continue to travel. It's certainly not easy sometimes, but there is help out there; inside of us too. There's a divine spark in each of us. We are all holy beings. On a holy planet. We might even be angels for all we know. Perhaps it's time we helped one another.

In chapter one, Benjamin's mother, Hanni Weiss, lights two white candles before the Friday sunset; to commemorate the beginning of the Jewish Sabbath. The Weiss family sit at their dining room table and prepare to take part in the Sabbath evening meal. They say the blessings over the wine and bread, and Hanni and her daughters serve everyone bowls of hot chicken soup. Thirteen-year-old Benjamin Weiss will celebrate his bar mitzvah the next morning. If you sit down and close your eyes . . . you might imagine yourself at the Sabbath table with them.

enjoy the story

H. J. Zeger

PART I

1

Hanni Weiss placed two Sabbath candles on a credenza, and she lit them with a wooden match. Her three daughters, Pearl, Zipporah, Raisel and youngest son, Herschel, watched while their mother placed her hands over her eyes and recited a Hebrew blessing:

"Blessed art Thou, O Lord our God, King of the Universe, who sanctified us by Thy laws and commanded us to kindle the Sabbath lights."

"Amen."

Hanni opened her eyes and waved her hands above the flames, drawing the devout illumination inward. She donned a white apron and returned to the kitchen with her older daughters, Pearl and Zipporah, who helped their mother prepare the Sabbath evening meal.

Raisel and Herschel sang and set the dining room table:

"Hava nagila, hava nagila, hava nagila ve-nismeḥa. Let's sing, let's sing, let's sing and be happy."

After Friday evening services, Mendel Weiss and his sons, Ignatz, Armin, Mordecai, and Benjamin, departed the great synagogue of Beregszász, and they happily walked home together. A crescent moon and stars provided them light as they passed the darkened shops on Main Street. Their route took them across a bridge above a river, through a tree-filled park, and then onto a cobblestone road where they lived. Bereg Street. Benjamin opened an iron gate for his father and brothers, and they walked through and approached the front door. Each of them touched a mezuzah on the doorpost before entering a three-story white stucco house.

On his way to wash his hands, Benjamin stopped to observe the brightly glowing candles on the credenza. He remained there while his father and brothers washed their hands.

"Go wash, Ben," his father said, before sitting at the head of the dining room table.

"Oh, I will, Papa."

Ben withdrew his eyes from the candlelight, and he quickly proceeded to clean his hands at the hand-washing area. Ben came to the table while Mendel's oldest son, Ignatz, lifted a decorative cloth that covered a sweet-smelling braided bread called challah; Hanni baked it specially for the Sabbath. The tall, dark-haired Ignatz stood and recited the blessing over the bread.

"Praised be Thou, O Lord our God, King of the Universe who brings forth bread from the earth."

"Amen," the family responded.

Hanni and her three daughters served steaming bowls of chicken soup. Parsley, sliced carrot, parsnip and long thin egg noodles that floated on top.

After Ben swallowed his last bite of chicken, he savored the apple pie Zipporah had baked. His mother poured her son a glass of sweet red wine; he drank, and it made him drowsy. He yawned while gazing at the flickering candle flames once more. Mendel proudly glanced over at his thirteen-year-old son.

"Why don't you go to sleep, Benjamin?" his mother said. "You have a long day tomorrow."

"I will, Mama."

Ben got up from the table, and he washed his silverware, glass, and plate in the kitchen. He came out to the dining room again, tousled little Herschel's hair, and then bid everyone a good night. The boy went upstairs, brushed his teeth, undressed, and then climbed into a bed he shared with his older brother, Mordecai. A strong wind knocked the window shutters against the side of the house as Ben closed a book and extinguished a kerosene lamp by the bed. He closed his eyes and fell into a deep slumber. The rest of the family retired soon after.

Downstairs, the remaining candlelight formed specter-like images upon the dining room walls and ceiling. Shadowy faces and distorted arms, hands and legs swayed in a macabre-like Sabbath dance. A powerful gust of wind blew in through the dining room window and knocked over a candlestick. The cotton cloth on the credenza burned. It rapidly caught the curtains on fire, and the blaze climbed the dry wood staircase to the second-floor bedroom. In the attic, Ben felt the heat singe his ears, nose, and eyelids. His bed sheets caught on fire while he heard his name called beyond the smoky sleep.

"Benjamin! Wake up. The house is burning!"

Someone shook Ben's arm, and he quickly sat up and opened his eyes.

There was no fire or smoke in the pitch-black bedroom in the attic. The wind had stopped, and the window shutters had become still.

"What's the matter, Ben?" Mordecai asked. "Who were you just talking to?"

"Nobody. I must have been dreaming—go back to sleep."

2

The rooster outside called while Ben's frightening nightmare replayed in his mind. He got out of bed, threw water onto his face from a washbasin, and then went down to the outhouse behind the barn. After relieving himself, he took soap and thoroughly washed his hands and face from a water spigot in the yard.

He returned to the bedroom and anxiously dressed for his bar mitzvah, donning a brand-new dark blue suit, white shirt, necktie, and a pair of glossy black shoes Mr. Jacob Katz, the shoemaker, had made for the occasion. Ben stood four feet ten inches and possessed a fit and limber body. He loved sports, especially soccer. An unusual birthmark on the outer side of his left nostril drew attention to a long and well-formed nose. Prominent cheek bones, large ears, and thin gentle lips accentuated his intense yet congenial face. He looked in the mirror and brushed his unruly chestnut-brown hair; his penetrating hazel-green eyes reflected back. The boy smiled as he tried on a black fedora that once belonged to his grandfather, Baruch Weiss. The hat was a little too big, so he put it aside. As he inspected the outfit his stomach felt like it was swarming with butterflies. Ben opened a gold-plated pocket watch that was handed down from father to son. It was half-past six, and a wintery gray daylight crept through a small window in the bedroom on the top floor.

Mordecai opened his eyes and grumpily asked, "What time is it, bar mitzvah boy?"

"Going on seven. I'll see you at the shul, brother."

"Sure."

Ben left the bedroom and walked down a flight of stairs, pausing outside his parent's bedroom door; he heard his father loudly snore from inside.

Downstairs in the kitchen Ben's mother tied the strings of an apron decorated with bright yellow daffodils. She and Raisel prepared breakfast while Herschel helped his older brother, Armin, feed a horse and milk a cow inside the barn. Afterward, they fed the chickens and a talkative rooster named Piros, a bright red and most annoying young bird.

"Breakfast is ready, Benjamin," Hanni called from the bottom of the staircase.

"Coming."

He turned from the bedroom door, came downstairs, and placed his suit jacket and a blue velvet bag on an armchair in the hallway.

"Good morning, Mama," the boy greeted, as he entered the kitchen.

"Morning, Ben."

"How do I look?"

Hanni straightened her son's blue-striped necktie. "You look handsome." She kissed his forehead. "Ready for your big day?"

"Ready as I'll ever be."

"Eat your breakfast. You want some coffee?"

"Please."

Hanni placed a plate of scrambled eggs and rye toast on the table. She poured a cup of coffee for her son.

"Is your father still sleeping?" his mother asked.

"Yes."

Raisel carried wood into the kitchen and stoked the cook stove. Ben watched as the flames jumped higher. She closed the iron plate on the stove top while Ben suddenly recalled the terrifying nightmare again.

"Eat your breakfast, Benjamin," his mother said, pulling him away from the dream.

"What's the matter?"

"I'm nervous about my bar mitzvah."

"You'll do fine. There's no sense in worrying about it," his mother stated.

"Oh, you're right."

Raisel filled a bowl with oatmeal and sat beside her brother. He sprinkled a generous amount of black pepper onto his eggs, and his mother sneezed twice.

"Gesundheit, Mamma."

"Thank you."

Ben scarfed down the eggs and a couple bites of toast. He pushed out his chair, got up, and drank the rest of his coffee standing.

"Why don't you finish your toast, Ben?" his mother asked.

"I don't have time."

"He doesn't have time," his mother quipped. "When did you become such an important man, Benjamin?"

He laughed and deposited his dirty dishes into the sink. The boy hurried from the kitchen and ran up the staircase, passing his father who was coming down the steps.

"Morning, Papa."

"Catching a train, Ben?"

"I'm going to the shul to practice my prayers."

"Best of luck today."

"Thanks, Papa."

Ben took a shortcut through the park, crossed a bridge, and arrived in the center of town. He quickly passed a market, a bakery, and the shop where Mr. Katz fashioned a variety of custom-made footwear and stylish leather handbags. The boy came to a building with grandiose architecture: the great synagogue of Beregszász. He reverently touched a silver-plated mezuzah that was nailed to the doorpost; he entered and covered his head with a white yarmulke before resting on a pew inside the main sanctuary.

With his prayer book in hand, Ben gazed at the lofty, blue-domed ceiling, enjoying the quietude of the chapel, he closed his eyes and meditated a few moments, sensing a mysterious presence above him. When Ben reopened his eyes, he suddenly saw a flutter of brilliant blue light on the domed ceiling. *What was that?* He picked up his skullcap which had fallen on the floor and returned it to his head. He looked up at the blue ceiling once more; nothing remained of what he had seen. Gold streaks of sunlight flashed through a stained-glass window high atop the eastern wall.

The cantor and the rabbi walked into the sanctuary, and they saw Ben deeply lost in thought.

"Ah, very good . . . the bar mitzvah boy has arrived early," Rabbi Schwartz announced.

"What's the matter, Benjamin? You look like you've just seen a ghost," Cantor Lexarman stated.

"Oh, good Shabbos," the boy greeted the two clergymen. And they firmly shook hands.

"We don't have much time, Ben," the cantor said. "Why don't we do a quick run through your Haftorah."

He and the cantor walked to the podium, where Ben unzipped his velvet bag and removed a black-and-white prayer shawl. He recited a blessing and kissed two ends of the long tallis. He wrapped the fringed garment around his back, neck, and shoulders while the red-bearded cantor performed the same ritual with his own prayer shawl. They sat and rehearsed some of the boy's prayers.

A buzz of excitement filled the sanctuary while Ben's mother and father entered the old building and seated themselves in a front pew. Their three daughters and four sons sat in the row behind them. Friends, relatives, and neighbors were all seated among the large congregation.

The cantor walked to the podium and sang the beginning of the Sabbath morning service, the Shacharit. Afterward, Ben stood on the bimah and read a portion of the Torah; his high-pitched voice rang through the sanctuary and spiraled up to the blue-domed ceiling, where unseen angels caught his devotions and delivered them up to God. Benjamin Weiss was no longer a boy that day, but a man. He ended his Haftorah and sat on a red velvet chair on the podium.

The talkative congregation chattered from their hard wooden seats. A baby cried as an elderly gentleman appeared near the podium; he requested silence by rapping on his hard-covered book. The mother carried the crying infant out of the sanctuary.

Rabbi Schwartz solemnly approached the lectern. He adjusted his long hanging tallis, turned and reassuringly smiled at Benjamin. The rabbi cleared his throat before delivering a lengthy sermon.

While Cantor Lexarman chanted the Musaf, the concluding part of the Sabbath morning service, Hanni admired the red roses on both sides of the podium; sunlight played upon their silky petals while Ben occasionally watched his mother's face glow with pride. His bearded and dreamy-eyed father stared up at the blue-domed ceiling, fondly recalling his own bar mitzvah in the very same sanctuary. Mendel turned a page and softly sang along to the final hymn of the service, the Adon Olam:

> The Lord of all did reign supreme
> before this world was made and formed.
> When all was finished by his will,
> then was his name as King proclaimed.
> And should these forms no more exist,
> He still shall rule in majesty.
> He was, He is, He will remain.
> His glory never shall decrease.
> And one is He, and none there is
> to be compared or joined to Him.
> He never began, and never will end.
> To Him belongs dominion's power.

> He is my God, my living God.
> To Him I flee when tried in grief.
> My banner high, my refuge strong.
> He hears and answers when I call.
> My spirit I commit to Him.
> My body, too, and all I prize,
> both when I sleep and when I awake.
> He is with me; I shall have no fear.

The prayer service ended, and Rabbi Schwartz reached for a silver wine goblet and a bottle from a shelf inside the lectern. He poured a small measure of sweet red wine, raised the cup, and recited the benediction: "Blessed are You, O Lord, King of the Universe, who has created the fruit of the vine."

The congregants responded, "Amen."

The rabbi had a sip of wine, then returned the bottle and the half-filled cup to the lectern. Ben exhaled a deep sigh of relief as the two clergymen approached him and shook his hand, extolling him with their heartfelt praises. The three men stepped off the podium, and the congregants and Ben's family members eagerly congratulated him.

Later that evening in the synagogue, Mendel and Hanni hosted a party celebrating their son's bar mitzvah. After they ate the main course, Mendel and his good friend Jacob Katz, the shoemaker, stood near a table with bottles of wine, whiskey, vodka, and schnapps. Cookies, cakes and fruit, as well as a stainless-steel coffee urn steamed on another table. Their wives sat nearby, chatting, eating a raison-nut kokosh, and drinking coffee. Mendel picked up a bottle of whiskey and poured some into two shot glasses. He and his friend lifted their drinks high and toasted:

"L'chaim, Jacob."

"And a mazel tov to your son," the shoemaker added.

"Thank you."

They drank and the fiery beverage warmed their insides. Mendel poured more whiskey.

Mr. Katz shook his head and deeply sighed.

"You know something, Mendel?"

"What's that?"

"I'm concerned about this hoodlum from Germany," Mr. Katz stated.

"Who are you referring to?"

"Klaus Von Hellmenz," Mr. Katz replied. "That loud-mouth bum in charge of the Nazi party. I heard him on my short-wave radio last night. He was giving a speech in Berlin. To a large crowd of his supporters."

"So . . . what did you hear, Katz?"

"He's a very charismatic speaker, apparently. My German isn't as good as yours, Mendel. But from what I understood, he doesn't like German Jews all that much. Or the Jews living in the rest of Europe for that matter. He kept on mentioning the final solution. *Die Endlösung der Judenfrage.*"

"I've heard about it," Mendel said. "He wants to rid all the Jews from Europe."

"And where does he want the Jewish people to live? On the moon."

Mendel laughed while his friend tilted the whiskey bottle and refilled their shot glasses again.

"I don't know about you, Katz, but I'm not buying any of Mr. Hellmenz' crazy propaganda. That worm should crawl back into the hole he came from."

"I completely agree with you, Mendel. But if the Communists aren't elected, that worm may become the new chancellor of Germany soon."

"Another fascist dictator Europe doesn't need," Mendel stated.

"My sentiments exactly."

"*L'chaim,*" the two men toasted once more.

After Mendel and Mr. Katz drank, they held each other's arm and slowly danced in a circle until they became dizzy and exhausted. The band ended its last song of the evening, and the three musicians—a male violinist, a man who played the piano, and a female accordion player who sang—left the stage and finally sat down to eat their dinner of brisket, potato pancakes, and vegetables.

Mendel and his friend poured themselves some coffee. Hanni eventually came over with her husband's overcoat and dignified top hat.

"Let's go, Mendel. Put on your coat. We're leaving," his wife said.

Mr. Katz frowned.

"We're going too," Ruth Katz announced.

Mendel protested, but to no avail.

"The night is still young, Hanni."

"The party is finished, Mendel. You both drank enough whiskey for two nights."

Hanni handed Mendel his top hat and helped him put on his overcoat.

"I'm terribly sorry, Jacob," Mendel said. "We must bid you and your dear wife a fond goodnight."

"Don't worry, Mendel. We'll have plenty more happy occasions to celebrate. Weddings for your daughters and a bar mitzvah for Herschel are yet to come. Which reminds me . . . I need to make Pearl and Zipporah high heels soon. They've become beautiful young women. Men are beginning to take an interest in them."

"Never mind their interest, Mr. Katz. Let's go, Mendel," Hanni said, as she tugged on her husband's arm.

"You too, Jacob," the shoemaker's wife nagged.

Mendel took out his wallet and paid the caterer and the band before he left.

"Mama, Papa," Ben greeted as the two couples congregated in the foyer of the synagogue.

Mr. Katz interrupted, "Ah, the bar mitzvah boy himself. And how does it feel to be a man, Benjamin?"

"It feels great, Mr. Katz. Thank you for asking."

"I'm happy for you."

"Are you riding home with us, Benjamin?" his mother asked.

"No, I'll be home later. My friends and I are going for a walk in town."

"Don't stay out too late, Ben," his father said, as he secured his black top hat and opened the large front door for his wife and Mr. and Mrs. Katz.

The two couples cautiously descended the synagogue steps to the sidewalk, where they bid each other a good night. Mr. Katz and his wife proceeded to their home close by, while Mendel and Hanni approached a horse and wagon parked alongside the curb. They observed a star-filled sky while Munka, the horse, clapped her hoof against the pavement and snorted a misty-white breath. With some effort, Mendel helped his wife onto the wagon and climbed up himself. He straightened his hat, shook the reins, and then made a clicking sound with his tongue. The strong, chocolate-colored mare trotted away from the shul and onto a main street paved with dull red cobblestones. The horse-drawn wagon traveled a kilometer or more, stopping on a bridge over the Verke River, the magical spot where Mendel proposed to his wife twenty-four years before. She entwined her arm around his and rested her head against his shoulder. They reminisced awhile as some bats flew overhead. Mendel gave the reins a shake, and the horse and wagon crossed over the bridge, into a park illuminated by faint orange gaslights. Brittle poplar leaves crackled beneath the horse's hooves; a sudden swirl of wind swept some yellow leaves into the air, and a solitary leaf landed on Mendel's coat sleeve unnoticed.

"You know, Hanni . . . we're not as young as we used to be."

"You're telling me?" his wife said, shivering. "Come on, Mendel, I'm cold."

He rattled the reins again, and Munka broke into a slightly faster gait. They left the gaslit park behind, along with their fond memories. The horse loped along a narrow lane and eventually stopped by Mendel's modest three-story stucco house. He drove through the open wrought-iron gate and parked near the barn; a half moon rose above its roof. He got off the wagon and helped his wife down. She brushed away the poplar leaf that stuck to her husband's coat sleeve. The bright moon-glow formed silvery-yellow halos around their heads. They embraced and kissed for a moment.

"I'll be in soon, Hanni. I have to take care of the animals."

"Don't be too long."

Hanni entered the house, pulled off her brown leather gloves and hung up her coat and scarf. She noticed an amber light shine from the library nearby; a fire burned in a hearth inside. Hanni poked her head through the doorway and saw her oldest son, Ignatz, was reading a book near the fireplace. Two kerosene lamps provided him additional light.

"Hello, sweetheart," his mother greeted the tall dark-haired man.

"Good evening, Mama. Papa in the barn?"

She nodded and went over to warm her strong but aging hands by the fire.

"You left the party early. What's the matter, Ignatz?"

"I wasn't feeling well."

"I'm going to make some hot tea with honey and lemon," his mother said, combing her fingers through her son's hair. "I'll bring you a cup."

Ignatz smiled and turned a page in the book. The light of the fire cast his tall shadow on the wall beside him.

Outside, Mendel unbridled the horse and brought her into the barn. He brushed her down, poured fresh water into two separate troughs; the horse and milk cow drank. Piros, the rooster keenly observed them from his roost. Mendel bid the barn's occupants good night. He carried a kerosene lantern out and closed the sliding wood doors. Before entering the house, he washed his hands under the water spigot in the yard.

Hanni placed two steaming cups of tea on the kitchen table. Her husband sat, added a spoonful of honey to his cup, and then stirred in a slow, deliberate manner.

"It's nice and warm in here," he said.

"Ignatz built a fire in the library."

"He's been awfully quiet lately."

"He's doesn't feel well."

"Oh?"

"I gave him aspirin and tea."

"Good. Benjamin did a magnificent job on his Torah reading this morning," Mendel said. "I'm proud of him. The rabbi's sermon was too long."

"They usually are," his wife said.

Seated opposite her husband, Hanni sipped the hot tea and thought about their oldest daughter, Pearl. She put down her cup and rubbed her arthritic hands.

"Pearl wants to go to America, Mendel."

He pretended not to hear his wife, staring out the kitchen window, and thinking of what he had to do for work the next day. He repeatedly drummed a spoon against his cup.

"Mendel?"

"*Igen*, Hanni?"

"Stop it. That's annoying me. Did you hear what I said?"

"Everybody wants to go to America someday."

"I didn't say everybody," Hanni stated.

"Who wants to go to America?"

"Pearl—."

"Sorry, I was daydreaming."

"You drank too much whiskey, Mendel."

"Oh, leave me alone already. I was celebrating. How many times will Benjamin have his bar mitzvah?"

He took his cigarettes from his shirt pocket and lit one. He reached for a Hungarian newspaper, the *Magyar Nemzet*. Mendel's dignified jaw locked as he blankly stared at the front page. A photograph displayed a man dressed in a full military uniform; his arm was stiffly raised; a red, black and white armband was tied around it. The man's face looked as if it had been bitten by a rabid dog. A headline was printed above the photograph:

Klaus Von Hellmenz Elected Chancellor of Germany

"Have you seen this yet, Hanni?"

"What?"

"That Nazi politician was appointed the new chancellor of Germany last night."

He showed her the unwelcome news on the front page.

"He has a scary looking face," she remarked.

"He doesn't look like a kindhearted man—that's for sure," Mendel said. He yawned and dejectedly folded the newspaper.

"I agree."

"What were you saying about Pearl?" Mendel asked. "She can't go flouncing off on vacation. Especially such a long distance from home."

"She isn't going on a vacation, Mendel. She wants to live in America."

"What for?"

"She doesn't like it in Beregszász anymore."

"I don't either," Mendel said. "Do you see me running off to America? And where does Pearl plan to live once she gets there?"

"In Newburgh, New York."

Hanni bit into a chocolate-filled kokosh she had saved from the party. Mendel lit himself another cigarette.

"Where is Newburgh, Hanni?"

"Your brother lives there. Near the Hudson River. She will stay at his house until she finds an apartment."

"Oh. And what will Pearl do for work in Newburgh? Someone will have to sponsor her. Then she'll need a green card. It's not that easy Hanni."

"I told you—your brother agreed to sponsor her. He mentioned it in the last telegram he sent us. Don't you remember?"

"Yes, I recall now," he replied.

Mendel sighed, drank some more tea, and then sucked on another cigarette.

"I wish you would stop smoking already. America is the land of opportunity. Your brother became successful there. And I heard that most of the houses have indoor plumbing now."

"And I suppose all the streets in America are paved with gold," Mendel said.

"Only the sidewalks. Don't be ridiculous, Mendel. Besides—if Germany starts another war—we may all have to leave Beregszász eventually."

"Those are only crazy rumors, Hanni. Germany is much too busy rebuilding their country from the last war. Does Zipporah want to go to America also?"

Tears welled up in the short but strong woman's brown eyes.

"I told her she couldn't leave home until she finished school."

"Oh, Hanni . . . don't cry. How fast our little girls have grown up."

"Our boys too," Hanni said, wiping her tears. "Why don't you go to bed, Mendel. You're probably exhausted. Where are you working tomorrow?"

"Jacob wants me to pick up some boxes from the leather factory, and I'll have to drive to Uzhhorod afterwards."

"For what reason?"

"A customer owes me money. I'll stop by Hugo's farm and bring back a few sacks of vegetables."

"Get some tomatoes and cabbage," his wife requested. "And take the lantern with you—you'll be coming home in the dark. I'll pack you a supper."

"When does Pearl plan to go to America?"

"When she has enough money saved for a ticket on the steamship," Hanni replied.

"How much does a ticket cost?"

"A one-way second-class ticket from Trieste to New York would be a hundred and sixty American dollars."

"Why a one-way ticket?" Mendel asked while he wrinkled his brow. He felt a sharp sadness pierce his heart.

"She's not coming back to Hungary, sweetheart."

"Oh?"

Tears rolled down Mendel's cheeks; he removed a handkerchief from the pocket of his dress shirt.

"Pearl will be okay, Mendel. Don't worry. She's a grown woman. And she speaks good English."

"I know. Where is Trieste?"

"On the northeast coast of Italy. She'll have to take a train from Budapest to get there."

Mendel pushed out his chair and tiredly stood; his balance was a little shaky.

"Pearl doesn't have to worry about the money, Hanni. I will buy her a first-class ticket. Where is Benjamin?"

"Still out with his friends. I'll stay up until he comes home."

"I'm going to sleep then." Mendel gently kissed the top of his wife's head. "Good night, sweetheart."

"Sleep tight, Mendel, I love you."

"I love you too."

note to the reader: Klaus Von Hellmenz is a fictitious name the author used to represent the Fuhrer of Germany during WW2. He chose not to use the Fuhrer's real name for personal reasons.

3

Five Years Later

In the summer of 1938, on a soccer field in Beregszász, Benjamin Weiss stood a few meters from the ball, faced the opposing team's goalkeeper, and then anxiously waited for a stripe-shirted referee to give him the signal for a penalty kick. A goal could determine the outcome of the amateur league soccer tournament. Ben placed his full attention on the ball while the goalie flapped his arms from side to side and up and down. There were only five more seconds left on the game clock before the match might go into overtime. The score was tied two-all between the reigning league champions, a flashy-colored and hot-shot team from Budapest, and a tough, dark-horse squad, the host from Beregszász. Ben played center midfielder for the underdogs. His team wore plain white tee shirts; black, white, or brown socks; and drab shorts of mismatched colors. Budapest's team flaunted navy-blue jerseys with muddied white numerals, gray shorts, white socks, and proper black athletic shoes. It was nothing short of a miracle that Beregszász had qualified for the quarterfinals, semi-finals, and now the finals.

Ben shut out everything around him while he took two deep breaths, dug his heels into the turf, leaned forward, and rested a hand on his knee; his adrenaline pumped hard. The other team's goalie smirked and waved a gloved hand at the penalty kicker. Ben wasn't fazed by his cocky distractions. The ref blew the whistle, and Ben sprinted for the ball. His timing was perfect; he kicked it straight for the goal at bullet speed. The overly confident goaltender thought he would easily catch or knock the ball away; at the very last moment it mysteriously swerved right and jumped past the goalie's hands and into the upper left corner of the net. Ben raised his arms high while the other team's goalie dropped flat on his face and angrily pounded his fists against the wet ground. The referee signaled the kick was good.

"Goal!"

The Beregszász fans and teammates on the bench hollered and jumped up and down. The game ended with looks of disbelief on the faces of Budapest's coach, players, and fans. Thunder sounded, and a light rain dropped onto the field. Ben's coach and teammates ecstatically mobbed him, lifted him onto their shoulders, and paraded him across the dampened turf. After the league's president awarded the Beregszász team the championship trophy, the defeated Budapest squad warmly congratulated them. The head referee patted Ben's muscular arm and gave him the game ball as a memento. Ben's father and Mr. Katz came down from the bleachers and approached the bench on the sideline.

"Great kick, Benjamin!" his father exclaimed.

"Yes—a wonderful goal," Mr. Katz stated. "Perfectly placed, if I may add."

Ben looked up while he untied his soccer shoes.

"Thanks . . . I prayed it wouldn't go over."

"God must have been listening to you," Mr. Katz said.

"Amazing kick, Ben," his team's goalkeeper said, as he offered him his hand.

"Thanks, Chubac."

"Think about what I told you before," the goalkeeper said as he looked deeply into Ben's hazel-green eyes.

"I will. See you at practice next week, Chubac."

"You won't. I'm joining the army," the goalie said.

"Oh. Good luck then."

"Thanks."

"Would you like a ride home?" Ben's father asked.

"Sure, give me a couple minutes, Papa."

"I'll see you two later," Mr. Katz said. "And give my regards to Hanni."

"And ours to Ruth," Mendel said. "Coffee tomorrow morning, Jacob?"

"*Igen*. I'll see you bright and early."

Mendel's old brown mare lazily trotted away from the athletic field, pulling the four-wheel wagon behind. Ben opened an umbrella and shielded him and his father from a steady rain. A clamorous railroad bell rang when they neared a crossing; the horse stopped well before the wooden barrier as a slow-moving freight train sounded its horn. Mendel's faithful horse neighed and shook her head up and down while an iron-black locomotive chugged past with its graffiti-smeared box cars.

"Munka, it's okay," Mendel reassuringly told the horse. "I have to admit, son, it looked like the game was going into overtime."

"Why? You thought the goalie had a save?"

"You fooled me for a moment. Any higher the ball would've hit the crossbar. I've watched you make that kick before. And not always with success."

"It's too bad Mama didn't see the game," Ben mentioned.

"Maybe next time."

"Hear any more news about the war, Papa?"

"The Germans invaded France and Belgium this morning."

"Oh?"

"I heard it on the BBC. From Katz's short-wave radio," Mendel said. "I hope we're not in danger."

The young man thought as he watched the freight cars roll past: *We should have left Hungary two years ago. There aren't any passenger ships leaving Europe now. Why were we so naive?*

Mendel looked at his son. "What was your teammate, Chubac, talking to you about earlier?"

"He told me the secret police are arresting and beating up Jews all over Germany. There's been a lot of anti Semitism lately. A synagogue was burned to the ground."

"Where?"

"Frankfurt," Ben replied. "They're putting Jews onto trains and taking them to forced labor camps. Some as far as Poland. Jewish businesses have been forced to close in many German cities. Hungary may not be safe for us anymore."

"Fucking bastards," Mendel said, as he lit a cigarette. Munka sneezed. "Why can't they leave the Jewish people alone?"

"I don't know, Papa. It's not the first time."

A string of boxcars passed the horse's nose while Mendel tightly clenched the reins with one hand and nervously smoked with the other.

"How does your teammate Chubac know all this information?"

"He gets the news firsthand . . . his uncle works at the German consulate in Budapest."

"Maybe it's time for the rest of our family to leave for America, no?" Mendel said.

"It's too dangerous crossing the Atlantic now," Ben stated. "German U-boats are sinking anything that floats. Even if we found a passenger ship to sail on . . . we'd be risking our lives."

"Perhaps we could take a boat from Greece?" Mendel asked. "And go to Palestine. Katz told me that many Jews from Hungary have gone that route. We could start a new life in the promised land."

"We'd have to travel through Italy to reach Greece," Ben replied. "That might've been possible a few months ago, but now that Italy has become an ally of Germany, I'm not so sure it's a good idea."

"Ah . . . I forgot about that. Eh, why should we even worry about it, Ben? The Germans don't dare invade Hungary. Our army is too strong. Besides, the war can't go on much longer. The American and allied forces will rip them to shreds like the last war."

"I hope you're right," Ben said, as the final box car and caboose pushed a wet air into their faces.

The railroad bell stopped clanging, and the wooden crossing bar went up. A Hungarian army truck drove past from the opposite direction. Mendel cast his burning cigarette away and carefully navigated the horse and wagon across the bumpy tracks, and onto the center of town. They slowly passed the great synagogue, the butcher shop, the tailor's window, the fish market, Jacob Katz's shoe store, and then Mendel stopped at the large brick post office on William Street. He climbed down from the wagon and splashed his work boots into a dark puddle.

"I have to pick up a package, Ben," his father said as his old work horse sadly looked up.

"Oh."

"You can give Munka an apple. I'll be back in a few minutes."

"Okay."

Mendel straightened his coat collar and adjusted his top hat before going inside the large brick building. He opened the door and immediately felt a strange premonition. He stood in a line behind an old woman who had a battered suitcase by her side. She looked back at him. Mendel smiled and tipped his top hat. The haggardly old woman frowned as she made the sign of the cross. She turned and faced the clerk's window again. Mendel shrugged.

Outside the post office, Ben grabbed two golden delicious apples from a covered box in the back; he offered the horse a yellow apple, and she leisurely chomped it down. Ben contemplated the horse's blue, melancholic eyes; she seemed to question him. *She looks as if she wants to tell me something important, perhaps only a horse would have a sense of knowing. I wonder what she's thinking about. Probably doesn't have many years left. She's old now. I was just a little boy when I first saw her. She was young and strong then. Papa was too.* Ben fondly stroked Munka's coat. He smelled her earthy equine odor and kissed her neck. He climbed back on the wagon, polished his apple and relished the fruit's sweet juice. The gray clouds partially dispersed, and the afternoon sunlight reflected in the rain puddles. A faint band of colors appeared in the sky.

"Tasty apple, hah, Munka?" Ben asked.

The horse snorted and tapped her hoof upon the red cobblestone.

Back inside the post office, Mendel heard the blond-haired mail clerk shout: "Next in line!"

Mendel approached the window.

"Identification," the mail clerk rudely requested.

Mr. Weiss handed over his identity card.

"Everyone knows me in Beregszász," he calmly stated.

The clerk silently scrutinized Mendel's identification card: he coldly looked up at him.

"I don't know you."

"Mr. Gotlieb usually works at this window. Is he on vacation?" Mendel asked.

"His job was terminated yesterday. Take your card. Jews will no longer be employed at the post office, or any other municipal jobs in Hungary for that matter. No more questions."

Mendel stood there bewildered. Once again, he felt a ghostly air rest above his shoulders. The sun shone through a large window, forming a strange white circle on the dark marble floor; Mendel stared at it a few moments. The postal clerk returned and placed on the counter a medium-size box and a white envelope with foreign postage stamps on it.

"Sign your name," the clerk demanded.

Mendel scribbled his signature and collected the mail. He quickly exited the building, placed the box under a tarp in the wagon and gave his son the envelope. Mendel climbed up, shook the reigns, and made a clicking sound with his tongue. The horse moved slowly. They rode back to Bereg Street in silence.

Back home, Ben excitedly entered the kitchen with the soccer ball tucked under his arm. He tossed the envelope onto the table while smelling a pungent aroma of food.

His mother greeted him from the stove. "Hello, Benjamin."

"Mama—we won the finals! I scored the winning goal. We beat Budapest!"

His mother kept stirring something in a large, cast-iron pot. She covered it, and said with no more ado, "That's wonderful, Benjamin."

Disappointed by her lackluster response, he awkwardly stood there, noticing his mother's wrinkled forehead and dispirited stance. Her face appeared to have aged since he saw her in the morning.

"What's the matter, Mama?"

"Nothing. Go wash up and get ready for supper."

"What are we having?"

"Stuffed cabbage. Where's your father?" she asked while peeling a cucumber.

"In the barn."

Ben's sister, Raisel, entered the kitchen with a laundry basket full of clothes she had taken off the line.

"Hi, Ben."

"Hi, Raisel."

"I watched the first half of your game. Did your team win?"

"Yes . . . three to two. I scored the winning goal on a penalty kick."

"Wow—that's terrific!"

"I'll tell you all about it after supper."

Mendel wiped his muddy work boots on a mat before taking them off at the front door. He entered the house, hung up his coat, scarf, and hat, and then greeted his wife in the kitchen.

"I get any calls, Hanni?"

"No."

Mendel picked up the stamped envelope on the table and saw who it was from.

"Mr. Katz sends his regards," he told his wife.

"That's nice."

"Ben's team won the championship, Hanni. He scored the winning goal."

"He told me when he came in," she said, cutting up a kohlrabi.

She bit into the hard vegetable, then gave her husband a piece. "What's that?" she asked, noticing the purple-and-white postage stamps on the envelope.

"Mail from America."

"From your brother?"

"No, Zipporah sent it," Mendel replied. "Should I open it?"

"Go ahead. I'm through cooking."

Hanni gave her husband a butter knife, and he unsealed the envelope. He removed the folded letter and handed it to his wife. She looked at it a few moments. Mendel sat and drank some cold coffee from the morning.

"*Nu* . . . what are you waiting for?" he asked.

"All right. Let me sit down first."

Hanni untied her yellow apron, sat, and then unfolded the one-page letter written in Hungarian. She discovered a crisp hundred-dollar bill inside a folded piece of newspaper. She happily showed the money to her husband. He smiled while his wife cleaned and adjusted her reading glasses.

Dear Mama and Papa,

I hope all is well there. Because of the war my letter was probably delayed a long time. It's bitter cold in Newburgh right now. We had two snowstorms in one week. Spring is around the corner, though, and the apple trees will be blossoming soon. Wish you could leave Beregszász and come to Newburgh, but that may not be possible until the war is over. Next month my citizenship papers should arrive. I'm so excited! I visit Pearl whenever I get the chance. She sends her love. My job in the pocketbook factory is going well. On one of my days off, a girlfriend and I went by train to Manhattan. We saw a show on Broadway and had dinner in a Jewish delicatessen. I never dreamed New York City would be so much fun. Crowds of people everywhere. And tall buildings they call skyscrapers. I felt like an ant. Your brother sends his regards, Papa. Hugs and kisses to all.

love
Zipporah

Hanni folded the letter and placed it back inside the envelope. She glanced at her husband's melancholic disposition. He turned away and reached for a cigarette while tears rolled down his face.

"What's the matter, Mendel—why are you crying?"

"I'm glad our daughters are happy in America. I only wish we could be there right now also."

"I know. Put away the money, Mendel. We'll eat soon. I'll be right back."

Hanni went out the kitchen door to the backyard, where Piros, the friendly old rooster, hobbled past her short, quivering legs; the bird quietly muttered to himself as a songbird rustled in an apple tree nearby. Hanni watched as a big apricot-colored sun dropped behind the barn. She buried her face in her hands and cried.

4

The drivers of a Hungarian army truck and a German military vehicle, a *Kübelwagen*, abruptly braked in front of a busy food market on a main street in Beregszász. Two Hungarian soldiers climbed off the truck while three Nazi soldiers got out of the other vehicle, and they noticed two ultra-orthodox Jewish men browsing through an outdoor fruit-and-vegetable stall. Yellow stars were sewn onto the men's long black coats while a strange fur hat known as a *shtreimel* covered their heads. The Hungarian soldiers entered the market to buy whiskey and cigarettes while the three stubble-faced Gestapo approached the two bearded Jews.

A blond and blue-eyed Nazi named Sergeant Heimlich, sharply addressed the two men with a heavy German accent, "*Hei!* What are you doing here, *Juden?*"

"Buying food for our families," the taller man answered. "*Iz das* a crime?"

"*Muterfucker!*" the sergeant shouted, "*Das iz verboten*! You are violating the curfew—you should be home."

A Captain Manheim added insult to injury. "Or in the ghetto where you belong. *Schmutzig Juden.* Shame on you."

The taller Jew remained calm despite being called a *dirty Jew*. He answered the soldier in a broken German and Yiddish, "I'm sorry but we did not know about a curfew. Please, let us buy some food then we will go directly home to our families. I have *acht* (eight) *kinder* and my wife to feed. My friend Shmeil has six *kinder* plus his *muter and fater.* Everyone is starving."

"*Nein!*" Sergeant Heimlich shrieked, as he knocked off the man's funny round hat and punched him in the nose so hard it bled. The man staggered backward but remained upright. He held a white cloth to his bleeding nose. The shorter Jew picked up, kissed, and brushed off his friend's black fur hat before giving it to him.

Customers nearby watched in shock as children and infants cried. The Gestapo laughed, and the owner of the market came out and forced a smile. He apologized to his customers, comforting the children by handing them lollipops, chewing gum and fruit-filled candy from Vienna.

"Now look what you've done, *Juden.* You've upset the *kinder,*" Captain Manheim gently spoke as he patted a little boy's blonde head. His mother quickly grabbed the boy's hand and walked away.

"*Schmutzig Juden.* You're both under arrest," the sergeant announced.

"But we didn't know there was a curfew," the shorter *Chasid* stated.

"Shut up your mouth, *Yid!*" a Nazi corporal named Wagner yelled.

The three Gestapo pulled the Jews to the middle of the sidewalk, where they took out barber scissors and hacked off the men's lengthy beards and side-locks. Before they continued with their business, inquisitive pedestrians and shop customers pitied or laughed at the humiliated Jews. The two Hungarian soldiers arrived and kicked the beardless men onto the back of the flatbed army truck. It was already laden with families from Beregszász.

"Take us to the next location," Captain Manheim ordered the driver of the Hungarian army truck.

"Jawohl, Capitan."

The army truck and German Kübelwagen jerked up and down the cobblestone street. The thirty-plus passengers on the flatbed truck knocked against one another and struggled to keep from falling off. The jeep-like vehicle and truck rambled over the Verke Bridge, through Gorky Park, and then onto a more rural Bereg Street. The Hungarian soldier waved his hand out the truck window and both vehicles stopped in front of a modest three-story stucco house. The Hungarian truck driver got out with his clipboard and approached the Gestapo captain.

"I know the owner of this house," he told Captain Manheim. "He used to deliver bags of produce to my brother's restaurant. My boy played on the soccer team with his son. They won the league championship a few years ago. Against Budapest," the Hungarian proudly stated.

"Oh, really?" the captain congenially asked while casually exhaling some nasty smelling cigarette smoke into the Hungarian's face.

"Do you want us to bring them out?" the soldier questioned the German.

"Nein! —we will take care of it," the captain snapped. "What's the owner's name?"

"Mendel Weiss, *Capitan.*"

"Mendel Veiss?" the captain said, his accent making the w sound like a V.

"Igen," the soldier affirmed in Hungarian.

"Drop this load off at the factory," the captain ordered. "And pick up more Jews afterwards. Come back in one hour. And don't be late."

"Jawohl," the Hungarian soldier said as he checked his wristwatch and climbed back into the smoke-filled truck cab. He snatched the whiskey bottle from the other soldier and had himself a drink. He pulled the gear shift and bounced the truck up and down the stone-paved lane. The two Hungarian soldiers laughed along the way.

The Gestapo trio climbed from the military vehicle and viewed

Mendel Weiss' well-kept residence behind a tall, wrought-iron gate. Sergeant Heimlich shot the lock off with his silver Lugar pistol, and a feisty old rooster screamed when it heard the loud pop; the horse neighed, and Mendel's dairy cow almost tipped over a bucket of milk Ben had filled only a minute before the soldiers arrived. His brother, Mordecai, hid himself under a haystack. Ben sprinted to the house.

Sergeant Heimlich smiled, holstered his pistol, and then kicked open the iron gate. The high-booted Gestapo leisurely strutted onto the sweet-smelling property. Captain Manheim unzipped his pants, pulled out his prick, and then pissed under a blossoming apple tree. He admired the pinkish-white flowers, while Sergeant Heimlich relieved himself onto Hanni's favorite rose bush. A near-sighted Corporal Wagner focused through his coke-bottle eyeglasses, curious to know what was inside the barn. He approached it.

Ben stood breathless after gently closing the kitchen door at the back of the house. His heart pounded.

"What was that noise, Benjamin?" his mother asked. "How come you haven't milked the cow yet, Ben? You know I have to make butter today."

"I did the milking. Soldiers are here."

"Oh my God. Where is Mordecai?" his mother asked.

"Hiding in the barn."

Mendel threw down his newspaper. "What happened, Ben?"

"Lower your voice, Mendel," his wife pleaded.

"Someone fired a gun," Ben announced in a whisper.

"Hungarian soldiers?" his father asked more quietly.

"I think they're Nazis," Ben replied. He wiped perspiration from his face. "They spoke German."

"God help us," his father whispered.

Raisel and her younger brother, thirteen-year-old Herschel, came downstairs in their pajamas.

"What's all the commotion about, Mama?" Raisel asked while Herschel peeked through the kitchen window.

"Soldiers are outside," Hanni replied.

"Quiet, everyone," Mendel ordered. "Get away from there, Herschel. Go upstairs with your sister and hide in the closet. And don't make a sound. Ben—go to the basement."

"I'll stay here with you and Mama."

"We have to remain calm," Mendel said. "Make coffee, Hanni. Our guests may be visiting us soon."

"*Igen.*"

Raisel and Herschel ran up the staircase.

Hanni poured hot water from the stove into her largest coffee percolator, while Ben took a broom and swept the hallway. Mendel lit a cigarette. And nervously opened the newspaper.

In the barn, a poor-sighted Corporal Wagner kicked away the rooster, and he accidentally stepped into a full bucket of milk, drenching his boot, sock and pants. He angrily swore at the cow in German, "*Verdammte Kuh!*"

Mordecai's underarms sweat profusely as he a drew a shallow breath beneath the hot scratchy haystack.

The captain entered the barn and looked down at the corporal's wet pants. "Did you piss your pants, Wagner?"

"That fucking milk pail was in the way!" he exclaimed as his face turned a bright pink.

"That was clumsy of you," the captain stated.

"I didn't see it."

"Perhaps you should get yourself some stronger lenses. Hey, Corporal?"

"I found a pump for water," the sergeant announced as he entered the barn. "What happened to you, Wagner?" the sergeant asked, noticing the corporal's dampened boots and trousers.

"He w*et his diaper,* Sergeant."

The captain and the sergeant had a good laugh, while the corporal kicked some hay and continued to curse.

I'm very thirsty," the captain stated. "Let's drink some water. And the corporal can change his diaper."

"*Ja, das ist gut,*"I am thirsty also," the sergeant said, still laughing.

While the three Gestapo gathered at the water pump in the

yard, Herschel and his sister secretly watched them from an upstairs window. The men pumped out cold water and drank. Afterward, the corporal removed his boots, socks, and stripped to his underpants. He washed his trousers and socks, then hung them on the clothesline nearby.

"I'm hungry," Captain Manheim announced. "There must be some food in the house. Shall we pay Mr. Veiss and his family a visit . . . hey, Heimlich?"

"*Ja . . . das ist gut.*"

Hanni nervously stood by the stove, where she fried potatoes, onions and garlic in a cast-iron pan. She sprinkled in paprika, salt and black pepper; she sneezed. Mendel nervously smoked at the kitchen table while he blankly stared at the headlines in the Magyar Nemzet newspaper.

"A German submarine was sunk in the North Sea, Ben," his father announced.

"Oh?" he replied, pensively sweeping the kitchen floor.

They heard a loud banging on the front door. It echoed through the house.

"That must be our guests," Mendel said. "Come in!" he yelled from the kitchen table.

Herschel and Raisel clearly heard their father's boisterous voice from upstairs. They shook inside the bedroom closet.

Modeling his white boxer shorts with his long black boots in hand, the corporal followed after the other two Nazis. They entered the home and observed a framed photograph on the wall in the foyer: Mendel, his wife, five sons and three daughters. The sergeant saw it, ripped it off the wall, and smashed the glass-covered picture under his boot. While the corporal investigated the library, the other two men stomped down the hall and gathered at the threshold of the kitchen. Ben and his father locked eyes with the men. The Gestapo observed the cleanly shaven father and son.

"Welcome to our humble abode, gentlemen," Mendel politely greeted in German. "The coffee is almost ready. Please . . . have a seat."

"*Danke schön*," the captain said.

"Can I help you with something?" Mendel inquired.

"Are you German?" the captain asked.

Mendel thought for a moment, looked at the captain, and replied, "No, we are Hungarians."

"And I assume you are Jews?" the sergeant interrogated in a much less friendly tone.

An uncomfortable silence filled the kitchen a moment. Mendel thought to say they were Christians.

Standing guard with the broom, Ben replied in a resolute manner, "*Ja*. We are Jews."

"I thought so," the sergeant said, as he approached the young man.

Ben clenched the broom handle with his powerful hands. A much taller Sergeant Heimlich loomed over him and glared into his piercing green eyes. The sergeant grabbed the broom handle and broke it in half. He took out his gun and placed the barrel against Ben's forehead. He asked if Ben spoke German, "*Sprechen Sie Deutsch?*"

"*Ja*."

"*Gut. Auf dem boden sitzen*," the sergeant said while pointing his gun toward a corner of the kitchen. Ben went over and sat on the floor as he was told.

The captain and the sergeant seated themselves at the kitchen table. They removed their boots while Hanni wrinkled her nose at the soldiers' foul foot odor.

"Give us coffee and breakfast! Schnell," Sergeant Heimlich demanded Hanni in German. The sergeant placed his pistol on the kitchen table. Hanni stood confused by the stove.

Ben translated, "Mama, he asked for you to give them coffee and make breakfast."

Hanni acknowledged with a meek 'yes' in Hungarian, "*Igen, Capitan*."

Mendel courteously offered the Gestapo his Marlboro cigarettes. He lit them with a silver-plated lighter.

"Ah, American cigarettes. *Danke schön,*" the captain said. "Where did you get those from?"

"My two daughters live in America," Mr. Weiss proudly replied. "They mail me sometimes."

"Wunderbar," Captain Manheim said.

Hanni served them two cups of coffee.

The sergeant turned to Mendel and gave him a dirty look. "We are from the Secret Police," he said. "We were informed that a Mendel Weiss owns this house. Is that you?"

"Yes, my name is Weiss. Why?"

"You and your family are under arrest," the sergeant announced.

"Have we committed a crime?"

"Shut up your fucking mouth, Jew-dog!" the sergeant shouted. He picked up his pistol and pointed it at Mendel. Hanni's heart almost stopped.

"Sergeant!" Captain Manheim exclaimed. "Don't be so rude. We are their guests. Put away your gun. And show them some manners. Corporal! There is coffee if you want."

Hanni browned some potatoes, then checked the beef brisket that was warming in the oven. She took down plates from the cupboard and forks from a drawer, then placed it all on the table. She cut into a challah that was left over from the previous Sabbath.

"Mendel, would you please ask the Capitan if I could get some fresh eggs from the barn."

"Capitan. Is it possible my wife can go to the barn for eggs?"

"Ja."

The captain nodded and gestured with his hand for her to go. Hanni took a small basket and quickly went outside through the kitchen door. She briefly noticed the strange pants and socks drying on the clothesline. She entered the barn and judiciously selected a dozen brown eggs. The rooster questioned her by pecking near her feet. Before leaving she glanced at the haystack and softly spoke:

"Mordecai? Are you there?"

"Mama?"

"Stay where you are. The Germans are in the house right now. They will arrest us. Don't come out until they leave."

"Where will they take you?"

"I don't know," his mother replied. "There's money hidden under the mattress in the attic. Take it and leave Beregszász tonight. Go to Budapest. It's safer there."

"Mama— "

"I have to go back inside the house now. I hope we will see you again, Mordecai."

The half-dressed corporal snooped around the living room and discovered a bottle of plum brandy. He drank some, took the bottle upstairs, and then ransacked the master bedroom. He searched through a dresser and found a meager amount of American dollars and Hanni's diamond wedding ring. He stashed it into his shirt pocket, gulped more liquor, and then threw the bottle into a mirror, breaking both. The loud noise frightened Herschel and Raisel, who were hiding in the closet across the room. They dared not breathe. Something fell from inside their hiding place. The corporal heard. He walked toward the closet, held onto a doorknob, and then flung open the door. Sunlight flooded in. The corporal threw the clothes off the hangers and saw two blurred figures tightly squeezed in a corner.

"Come out!"

The sister and brother crawled from the hiding place on their hands and knees; they slowly came to their feet and raised their arms above their heads in surrender. The corporal lasciviously rolled his beady eyes over the young woman's firmly shaped body. He turned his gaze to the frightened thirteen-year-old.

"Go to the kitchen," he sternly ordered him in Hungarian.

"Igen, *Capitan.*"

The corporal ripped off Raisel's pajama top, exposing her shapely breasts. She tried to scream, but nothing came out of her mouth. He clumsily fondled her breasts while attempting to kiss her. She smelled his raunchy breath as he took out his semi-erect penis and pushed her onto the bed. He was about to climb on top when the captain yelled from the bottom of the staircase: "Wagner! Come down for breakfast. We're leaving soon."

The corporal returned his flaccid member to his boxer shorts, and he awkwardly put on his coke-bottle eyeglasses.

"Get dressed!" he ordered the trembling young woman.

5

While Hanni, Raisel, and Ben washed the pots, dishes and silverware, the captain got up from the table and announced, "I'll be back in ten minutes. I have to take care of something urgent."

"Do you need my assistance, *Capitan?*" the corporal asked as he smeared some butter onto a slice of challah.

"I'm going to take a shit. You want to watch me?"

"*Nein, Capitan.*"

Ben, his father, and the sergeant burst out laughing.

"Have the older son and his sister pack some clothes for everyone, but not too much," the captain ordered, as he was about to leave for the outhouse.

"*Jawohl.* Go upstairs and pack," the sergeant told the brother and sister.

They went upstairs and placed some of their family's belongings onto bed sheets and tied them into bundles. Raisel threw a bra, panties, her favorite dress, and a pair of high heels into a ragged suitcase, and she secured it with twine. The brother and sister carried the packed clothes down to the living room, where they glumly looked at each other.

"I'm really afraid, Ben."

"Me too, Raisel."

"Shut up!" the sergeant yelled, as the Gestapo gathered the whole family into the living room.

The Hungarian army truck pulled up front; the driver beeped the horn as the other soldier tipped the whiskey bottle and drank.

"Get them out of here, Wagner," the captain ordered.

Fully dressed, the corporal held his pistol firmly aimed at Ben's back. He led the family out the front door, toward the flatbed truck. Mendel recognized one of the Hungarian soldiers and waved to him, but the soldier sadly looked away and climbed behind the wheel.

Ben briefly glanced at the barn before helping his family members onto the flatbed truck. Various passengers knew the Weiss family, and they somberly greeted them.

"Is that everyone, *Capitan?*" the Hungarian soldier asked from the driver's seat.

"*Ja*—now take them directly to the brick factory," the captain replied, noticing the soldiers' slapdash condition. "And this will be your last run of the day. Both of you need to sober up."

"*Heil Hellmenz.*"

The army truck jerked forward suddenly and stalled twice. It rocked up and down Bereg Street while Mendel and his family dismally watched their home disappear. The old red rooster stood beside the front gate and crowed long and loud. The Gestapo left.

The army truck slowly approached a bridge over the Verke River. An old man waved from inside a small fishing boat.

"Where are they taking us, Papa?" Raisel asked.

"God only knows, sweetheart. I'm sure it will only be temporary."

"Who will feed and give water to the animals while we're gone?"

Dream-like, Raisel's father replied, "Hopefully one of our good Christian neighbors will look after them. For now, we have enough to worry about."

Raisel and her mother cried while Mendel securely held onto their arms.

When the army truck approached the great synagogue of Beregszász, Ben saw that its colorful stained-glass windows had been broken. Curse words were painted on the front facade in German and Hungarian. Ugly black swastikas had been smeared on the large wooden doors. Long benches, tables and chairs, and the ark for the Torahs had been busted up and stacked on the sidewalk for firewood. Torah scrolls, books, and prayer shawls were thrown in disheveled piles beside the broken furniture. Young, snot-nosed children curiously picked through the mess; one of them mockingly wrapped himself in a prayer shawl and ran down the street with it. The other gentile kids glanced up when the army truck parked in front. A soldier got out and entered the shul. He appeared shortly after, pulling the rabbi by his beard; he still wore his tefillin and prayer shawl. His wife cried by his side as they were put onto the truck.

The army vehicle crossed over some railroad tracks and approached an athletic field overgrown with weeds and tall grass. Ben sadly observed the place he had played soccer from the time he was a little boy. The driver turned onto a one-lane dirt road, beeping the horn for a group of pimple-faced children who laughed and waved while some older, mean-faced boys threw stones at the passengers on the back of the truck. Ben recognized the Beregszász brick factory from a distance; he had been there a couple of times with his father to deliver sacks of clay. The building had no outer walls; only pillars and beams supported its flat roof. Railroad tracks ran adjacent to the factory. The army truck stopped in front, and the two Hungarian soldiers drunkenly climbed out and shouted at the people on the back.

"Get off, *Juden!*"

Ben helped his family members from the truck, then he and some other young men assisted the children and elderly.

"I said move!" a soldier yelled once more.

Meanwhile, another Hungarian soldier prodded an older gentleman who was wrapped in a blanket and fast asleep.

"Get up, you fucking rotten Jew-dog-bastard!"

The old man mumbled an obscenity but remained stationary. The soldier yanked him off the truck and dropped him onto the hard ground. The old man screamed as the soldier repeatedly kicked him in the ribs; someone else came along and beat him with a wooden club till he stopped breathing. Two civilian-clothed men grabbed the old man's limbs and carried him to a garbage-strewn field nearby. They dropped him into an open grave, where several other bodies rested. Shortly thereafter several young men filled the hole with shovelfuls of dirt. And that was that.

Mendel and his family entered the already crowded brick factory. Ben saw a teammate from his soccer team, a few neighbors, and his boss from the glass shop. Everyone was corralled inside like sheep. Men, women, older children read from prayer books, as if they were in the synagogue, chanting hymns, beating their chests and crying out loud. Ben caught a glimpse of Cantor Lexarman, the clergyman who had officiated at his bar mitzvah several years ago. He stretched his neck, but the cantor's troubled eyes and long reddish gray beard soon vanished within the crowd.

"It stinks in here," Hanni said, wrinkling her brow and holding her nose.

Raisel helped her mother walk.

"I see Mr. Katz," Ben announced. "There's room for us next to them."

"Let's go," his father said.

Ben took hold of his father's arm as they neared the shoemaker and his wife. The couple were seated on the dirt floor; a blanket was draped over Mrs. Katz; she coughed and shivered. Mendel and his family awkwardly approached them. Mr. Katz's wife momentarily opened her eyes, barely managing a faint hello and a brief smile.

"Hello, Jacob," Mendel sadly greeted.

"Mendel, Hanni, Ben, Raisel, Herschel. I'm so happy to see you all," Mr. Katz said. "You just arrived?"

"A little while ago," Mendel replied. "When did you get here?"

"Last night. Sit, everyone. Where is Mordecai and Ignatz?"

"Mordecai was hiding in the barn when they took us away," Ben replied. "We don't know where Ignatz went."

"May God protect them from these terrible monsters," Mr. Katz said.

"Your wife doesn't look so well," Mendel stated. He smelled a urine-like odor close by.

"We slept on the floor last night," Mr. Katz said. "It was cold. Ruth caught a chill. I pray she doesn't have a pneumonia."

Raisel bent down and felt the woman's forehead. "She has a temperature. Do you have any medicine?"

"A few tablets of aspirin," Mr. Katz replied. "I'm going to look for a doctor while there's still daylight." He stood and brushed the dirt off the seat of his pants. "Stay here and rest, everyone."

"I'll go with you," Ben said.

Raisel gave her brother a near empty hot-water bottle.

"Try to find some water, Ben."

While the two men threaded their way through the populated brick factory, Ben stopped briefly to check the time inside his gold-plated pocket watch. It was three o'clock. He closed the cover and carefully placed it into his pants pocket again.

"What time is it, Benjamin?"

"Three."

"Has anyone seen a doctor?" Mr. Katz inquired.

"We need a doctor!" Ben called.

"There may be one on the other side," someone mentioned, and pointed toward the direction.

Ben and Mr. Katz walked between a group of Jews wearing long black coats and round fur hats. Without interrupting their prayer chants they glanced at the two men.

"Where were you arrested?" Ben asked.

"At my shop last night. Ruth turned on the light by mistake. We just came from the market when the Gestapo burst through the door. Ruth got so scared she wet herself and dropped the groceries on the floor. They stole what little money we had in the cash register and smashed everything in the shop, including the store front window. Bastards! My poor wife managed to salvage a couple of carrots and one onion before they took us away. That's what we have to eat tonight. Carrots and onion. And there's no place to cook here."

"Fucking Nazis," Ben muttered. "They should all turn into maggots and rot in the earth."

"Careful what you say around here, Ben. My sentiments exactly but the Hungarian army may be even worse than the Germans. Last night I spoke to a man who escaped from a ghetto like this in Munkacs. He told me he saw Hungarian soldiers beat people to death there. And rape young women and girls. We aren't in a safe place my friend. There's not much food here. And the living arrangements are atrocious. As you can see."

"How long do you think we'll be here?"

"I'm not sure," Mr. Katz answered. "Anyone know a doctor? A train may be coming in a few days. Someone said it will take us to a labor camp."

"You know where?"

"No. But I hope it's better than this shithole."

"Is there a doctor in the house?" Ben shouted. "We need a doctor. Does anyone know a doctor?"

The two men noticed an elderly woman who was washing her feet and socks with a water hose.

"There's some water," Ben said. "I'll wait until she's through."

A man called out nearby, "Who needs a doctor?"

"I do," Mr. Katz replied.

He turned around and saw a tall man dressed in a tattered blue suit, wrinkled gray necktie, and a pair of shiny black wingtip shoes. The man held a satchel, and a stethoscope dangled from his neck. Mr. Katz stared at him, gazing down at his polished shoes a moment.

"Thank God, you're just the man we've been looking for."

"Aren't you Jacob Katz, the shoemaker?"

"I am."

"I thought so. I'm Dr. Cornblooth. You made these shoes for me a couple years ago. Remember?"

Ben filled the water bottle nearby while the two men spoke.

Mr. Katz looked down at the doctor's shoes, which were made from fine Italian leather. A light bulb shone above his head.

"Oh, yes!" the shoemaker exclaimed. "Now I recall. You came to me when I had my shop on William Street. How are you, my old friend?"

"Fine . . . but I think the shoes you made me are holding up much better than I am."

Mr. Katz smiled as the doctor managed a chuckle.

Ben came over with the water bottle in his hand.

"Ben, this is Dr. Cornblooth," Mr. Katz said. "May I introduce you to my good friend and neighbor, Benjamin Weiss."

"Hello, Mr. Weiss."

"Nice to meet you, Doctor."

"Likewise."

"My wife is ill. She may have a pneumonia," Mr. Katz informed the physician.

"Take me to her. I have some medicine in my bag."

After the three men found their way back, the doctor knelt beside Mrs. Katz and took her temperature. He removed the glass thermometer from her mouth and read it.

"What's your prognosis, Doctor?" Mr. Katz inquired.

"She has a high fever. You were correct. It is pneumonia."

"*Oy vey ist mir*," the shoemaker moaned.

The doctor prepared a syringe with a small amount of penicillin. He wiped Mrs. Katz's exposed buttock with a cotton ball soaked in alcohol and injected the medicine. He placed a bandage on her skin, covered her buttock, and reached into his bag, handing Mr. Katz a small bottle of white pills.

"Give her two every four hours. Preferably with food. If you can find any that's edible."

"All right," Mr. Katz said, offering to pay the doctor.

He waved his hand, refusing to take the Hungarian currency.

"I don't want your money, Mr. Katz. Main thing your wife should feel better soon."

"I'm grateful for your help, Dr. Cornblooth."

"You're welcome. *zie gesunt,* everyone . . ."

Back on Bereg Street, Mordecai crawled from beneath the scratchy haystack. He stood and brushed himself off. He could barely see it was so dark now. He quietly found his way out of the barn, pumped water, and thirstily drank.

6

The squalid living conditions in the brick factory had grown much worse since Ben had arrived five days earlier. He sat up and eyed the dark rigid figures sleeping upon the dirt floor. It spooked him. His back hurt as he tiredly put on his dress shoes and tied the laces. He stood, got his balance, and carefully stepped over the sleeping bodies. He slowly made his way toward the latrine outside, a long and narrow ditch about a meter in depth. It buzzed with flies. He pulled down his pants and relieved himself.

A bright beam of light cut through the dawn mist. A train approached. Ben stayed clear of the railroad tracks as he observed the oncoming locomotive. It hauled a chrome dining car, two cars with sleeping compartments and seats, and a long line of boxcars. The train came to a full stop. The sun emerged, reflecting off the chrome dining car while inquisitive boys and girls ran up and gathered beside it, rubbing their dirty hands against the smooth cold steel. A Hungarian soldier yelled at them, and they ran away.

Ben returned to his spot and saw that his father was gone, his mother, sister, and brother still asleep. Mr. Katz worriedly sat beside his wife, who was coughing and reclining on her side.

"A train just arrived," Ben announced to Mr. Katz.

"I heard. Good morning."

"Morning. How's your wife doing?"

"A little better."

"You have more pills?" Ben inquired.

"A few but our water supply is dwindling fast."

"I'll go and see if I can find some water and bread," Ben said. "Where's my father?"

"He went up to pray about twenty minutes ago."

"Oh."

Ben took the water bottle and threaded his way through the crowd. He found a line and stood behind a young mother who rocked a pale-skinned infant boy in her arms; he cried incessantly. The young mother's dirty blouse was torn at the shoulder and her bra strap was exposed. She turned around and faced Ben, noticing the hot-water bottle in his hand. She held out an empty metal soup can.

"Can you spare some water?" the mother asked.

Ben filled the can halfway. She drank a little then moistened her baby's mouth by dripping some from her cracked lips.

"Thank you."

"You're welcome."

She turned away from Ben, unfastened her blouse, and then breastfed her son. The baby finally stopped crying. The line moved a little faster. Ben opened his watch and saw it was ten o'clock. He had been waiting on the line for almost two hours. He noticed a sudden rush of movement in the crowd. It got noisy. The disquiet in the factory prevented him from hearing the locomotive engine start up. The mother and her infant son finally reached the front of the line. There wasn't much food in the pot, only a grimy soup on the bottom. The mother grabbed a few slices of stale rye bread from the table. Ben did the same. He refilled the hot-water bottle from a hose nearby. The woman gently placed her baby on the ground and prepared to wash him. People around them moved in a frenzy.

"What's going on?" Ben asked an elderly man.

"The train. It will leave soon. Hurry."

"Are you coming?" Ben asked the young woman who was washing her baby's behind.

"No."

Herschel and Raisel helped Mrs. Katz stand, as both families prepared to make their departure from the brick factory ghetto. Hanni worried herself sick for Ben, but she finished organizing their clothes and meager belongings. Raisel wrote a note for her brother and placed it on the top of his clothes bundle. She secured the note with a piece of broken brick.

"Ben is gone a long time, Mendel. I'm worried what happened to him."

"We have to go—we can't wait much longer, Hanni."

A Hungarian soldier yelled twice, "Start moving toward the train! Move toward the train!"

Mendel recognized the soldier; he was the coach of the soccer team Ben played on a few years before.

"Mr. Szalasi, it's good to see you again. I'm Mr. Weiss. Ben's father. He scored the goal for the championship. Against Budapest."

"I don't know you!" the soldier shouted, as he prodded Mendel with the end of his rifle.

Hanni tearfully looked up at the Hungarian soldier. She inquired, "Our son has gone for food and water. He won't be too long."

"Go! Before I beat you, old woman."

Mendel held onto his wife's arm while avoiding any more eye contact with Mr. Szalasi.

"I'm a hundred percent sure he was the coach of Ben's team," Mendel stated. "Come, Hanni. He will catch up to us later."

Ben cringed when he found everyone had left the temporary dwelling. Maybe I have the wrong spot, he said to himself. He noticed his bundle of clothes and the note on top. He quickly read it:

> *Ben*
> *We waited for you, but we had to go.*
> *See you on the train, sweetheart.*
> *Love you*
> *Raisel*

Ben grabbed his bundle and followed the crowd toward the box cars.

Captain Manheim and Sergeant Heimlich stood like vultures on top of a raised wooden platform; they supervised the evacuation of the factory.

"They're not moving fast enough, *Capitan*" the sergeant stated. "At this rate we'll be here all night."

"I see. *Das ist nicht gut.*" The captain shouted through a megaphone: "Everyone get into the boxcars. Schnell!" He lowered the megaphone. "It would please our Führer if we shot them all right now. Hey, Heimlich?"

The sergeant laughed and crassly answered, "I could use the target practice."

"Oh, really?"

Both men lit cigarettes while Captain Manheim noticed that the unruly crowd had grown more reluctant to board the train. Some outright refused.

"Here—why don't you use my pistol—Heimlich?" Captain Manheim's candid suggestion caught the sergeant off-guard. Heimlich took a couple of nervous puffs and exhaled.

"What? To shoot someone?" the blond-haired sergeant asked.

"Let me see if you can hit the old man with the long white beard. The one in the black coat and round fur hat. He's holding the red suitcase."

"Is this a joke, Capitan?"

"*Nein.* It's an order," he said, handing the sergeant his semi-automatic Luger pistol.

"He looks like a rabbi to me," the sergeant spoke.

"So what? Go on, Heimlich. Shoot him. I'll wager you a beer, two whiskeys, and a hundred deutsche marks if you can hit him in the head. I'll give you two tries. If you miss—you walk to Austria—agreed?"

"Agreed," the sergeant reluctantly said, sealing the bet by shaking hands with his commanding officer. "Is it loaded?"

"Of course, but take off the safety first."

The sergeant centered himself and took two deep breaths. He

confidently aimed the pistol and pulled the trigger. The bullet raced for its target, making a hole in the old man's hat and knocking it off. While the man lifted his hand up to his head, the sergeant fired a second time. The orthodox Jew fell over backwards, and a pool of blood soon formed. People screamed and madly rushed past the dead man to get inside the box cars.

"Excellent shot, Heimlich. They're moving faster now."

"*Danke schön, Capitan.*"

"*Bitte schön.*"

The sergeant's gut wrenched as he handed the warm pistol back to his superior officer. It was the first time he had ever killed someone.

"I'm surprised you could shoot so well," the captain mentioned. "I owe you a few drinks tonight, Heimlich. Here's your money. Count it."

"*Danke.* I was one of the top three marksmen in the military academy, I attended."

"Ah . . . that explains it."

With the replenished hot-water bottle in his hand, Ben squeezed into a boxcar and sat on his bundle of clothes. He gobbled a couple bites of stale bread, drank water, and then anxiously waited for the train to move.

"Mendel Weiss? Hanni? Raisel? Herschel? Mr. Katz? Are you in here? It's Benjamin."

There was a brief silence.

"I am Mr. Katz," an elderly sounding gentleman spoke. "Who are you?"

"Ben Weiss."

"My name is Joseph Katz."

"Oh."

"*Zie gesunt,* Ben."

"You as well, Mr. Katz."

The brick factory had been emptied of all its occupants, except for the dead and those too sick or crippled to stand. The Hungarian army would shoot them in the morning.

The setting sun flickered through the open building; Corporal Wagner addressed Captain Manheim on top of the raised platform.

"That's everyone, *Capitan*."

"*Gut*."

Manheim raised the megaphone and ordered the Hungarian soldiers to close and bolt the boxcar doors. He and the sergeant climbed down from the platform and schlepped their duffel bags through the garbage-strewn factory.

"Let's get out of this pigsty," the captain said. "I miss my wife and kinder. Do you have a family—Heimlich?"

"*Nein*."

The two men pinched their noses closed while the setting sun cast their grim shadows along the dirt floor.

"How long is it to Munich, Sergeant?" the captain asked.

"It's about twelve hours to Mauthausen. Germany should be another three hours from there. If everything goes according to schedule."

The two Nazis boarded the train and found the car with the sleeping compartments.

"Take the top bunk, Sergeant," the captain ordered, as he set his duffel bag on the bottom mattress. "Let's find ourselves a nice comfortable seat in the dining car. We have a long ride ahead of us."

7

With his back pressed against the wall inside the boxcar, Ben felt the train suddenly move forward and finally roll away from the brick factory. It crept down the tracks like a gigantic iron millipede while Ben had another gulp of water before handing the rubber container to someone beside him. The train approached an impoverished neighborhood on the outskirts of town, where stinking garbage burned inside large, metal barrels. Behind their clapboard homes, soot-faced Gentile children happily played near the railroad tracks; they observed the oncoming train through a dusky light. They waved and shouted hellos to the engineer sitting high up in the locomotive; he waved back. Unaware of the human cargo inside the oxygen-deprived cattle cars, the youths counted each one as it passed, until the caboose finally arrived. The train horn blew in the distance, and the soot-faced Gentile children walked home in the dark, drumming their sticks against the smoking trash barrels. The Nazi locomotive engineer carefully opened a small vial, snorting a white powdered substance.

Ben maneuvered his cramped body while a woman in the boxcar somehow managed to light two stunted Sabbath candles.

She tearfully recited the blessing. And there was light. Only for a minute. A group of orthodox Jews sang a Sabbath evening prayer by heart. Ben and some others sang along with them:

> Beloved, come, the bride to meet.
> The Sabbath Princess let us greet
> For it is blessing's constant spring
> Of old ordained divinely taught
> Last in creation, first in thought
> Beloved, come, the bride to meet
> The Sabbath Princess let us greet
> Arouse thyself, awake and shine
> Thy light has come, the light divine
> Awake and sing, and over thee
> The glory of the Lord shall be
> Beloved come, the bride to meet
> The Sabbath Princess let us greet
> Crown of thy husband, come in peace
> Let joy and gladsome song increase
> Among His faithful, sorrow-tried
> His chosen people, come, O bride
> Beloved, come, the bride to meet
> The Sabbath Princess let us greet.

A child screamed on the other side of the car, and someone urinated into a wooden bucket near the center of the compartment. Ben had to go also, but he held it in. He closed his eyes and silently prayed. The candles burned out.

German officers and soldiers seated themselves at tables and enjoyed the comfort of the sleek, stainless-steel dining car. The men's raunchy-smelling cigar, pipe, and cigarette smoke thickened the air like a French chef's roux. They voraciously ate plates of schnitzel, sauerkraut, peas, and potato. And washed it down with a refreshing Hungarian spring water, Riesling wine, dark beer, whiskey, and Liebfraumilch. The train bumped along the rails, vibrating plates, glasses, and silver upon the white linen tablecloths. The bartenders and waiters nibbled on bites of food between their serving duties. A bow-tied busboy carried away the soldiers' licked-clean plates while a waiter named Otto took the Captain Manheim's, Sergeant Heimlich's and Corporal Wagner's dessert orders.

"Ice cream or fruit cocktail, Capitan?"

"I'll have the fruit cocktail, *bitte.*"

"For you, Sergeant?"

"Three dark beers and two more whiskeys *bitte,*" he replied, slipping the waiter 20 German marks. "Your service was excellent, Otto."

"*Danke schön.*"

"*Bitte schön.*"

"Would you like a dessert, Corporal?"

"Vanilla ice cream," he replied, peering through his inch-thick eye lenses.

Captain Manheim wiped his mouth and hands with a cloth napkin before reaching into his shirt pocket for a deck of playing cards.

"Anyone up for a game of poker after desert?"

"Do you have chips?" the sergeant asked the captain.

"*Ja,* I will go get them. They're in my duffle bag."

Sergeant Heimlich smiled. "My favorite card game. I'm in. Will you be joining us, Wagner?"

"*Ja.*"

The long train chugged ahead while bells chimed at a railroad crossing. Ben was awakened by a sensation of pins and needles shooting through his hands, legs, and feet. He asked the person next to him, "Do you know where we are?"

"It's probably a big city," replied a man squinting through a hole in the boxcar's metal wall. He saw what looked like the headlights of a car. They heard trolley bells, music, and loud laughter.

"Budapest," Ben said.

"Perhaps."

The train slowly approached a station; its wheels squealed to a halt. From the lighted platform, a Hungarian trainman announced in a boisterous voice, "Budapest! Budapest Station!"

A cluster of German and Hungarian troops milled about the station, while a much larger group of prominent Hungarian Jewish families waited with their fashionable handbags and suitcases. The group was excited to board the newly arrived train. Some of them were doctors, lawyers, teachers and professors, businessmen, women, politicians, and clergymen. Husbands and wives accompanied by infants, children, and teenage sons and daughters. Romantic newlyweds kissed on benches. Several poorer-looking families bleakly stood nearby; their meager belongings bundled in white sheets and pillowcases. Those parents argued with each other while their babies cried for milk, or diaper changes.

Ben placed his ear against the boxcar and clearly heard the infants' wails.

Although the evening wasn't a particularly cold one, the well-to-do women on the station platform had dressed in fine wool skirts, mink coats, dressy leather boots, white gloves, and feathered bonnets. Their diamond jewelry sparkled in the yellow lamplight. The gentlemen wore the latest style boots and shoes, silk ties, tailored suits, and black felt top hats. They casually draped their tweed overcoats and double-breasted suit jackets over their arms and shoulders while their young daughters held dolls, and little boys excitedly gripped red rubber balls. The children and adolescents were also dressed in their Sunday best.

When the wealthy Hungarian Jews purchased their first-class tickets, the travel agency had told them their fare included a full-course dinner and breakfast, plus private sleeping compartments for them and their children. The travel agent had also promised that—when the passengers reached their destination—they would be housed at ski resorts in the neutral Swiss Alps—far from the imminent dangers of war. And the travelers' lodging and meals would be paid courtesy of the German government.

Hungarian soldiers opened the doors of three empty boxcars.

Large black capital As and Ds had been painted on the sides of the cars. Soldiers first guided the impoverished families into the empty cars, filling the cars three-quarters full. The affluent group of Hungarian Jews watched the poorer families and felt sorry for them.

A tall, well-dressed woman on the platform argued with one of the Hungarian soldiers. In her high heels she stood a foot taller than the soldier. He pointed toward the boxcar with the capital *A* painted on it. "Get inside," the soldier ordered the affluent couple.

"There must be some mistake," the high-heeled woman told him. "I'm sure it's a mistake. My husband and I only travel in first class."

She showed him their tickets. The Hungarian soldier scowled.

"First class? Are you Jews out of your fucking minds? Get inside now!"

The high-heeled woman and her husband smelled a nasty odor coming from inside the metal compartment. The soldier pushed the woman, and she started screaming hysterically. Others watched, and they also refused to board. Her husband raised his fist, ready to strike the soldier.

"What's going on here?" asked a German soldier regarding the dispute.

"This couple won't board the train."

"Why not?"

"They claim to have first-class tickets," the Hungarian soldier replied.

"First-class tickets?" The Nazi laughed.

"*Ja.*"

In defense of his wife, the woman's husband told the Nazi that they would not travel in a filthy cattle car and paid good money for the tickets.

"Good money? Let me see those tickets," the Nazi requested.

The wife handed them over.

"These tickets are indeed for first-class accommodations, but unfortunately all the first-class seats and sleeping compartments have been given to military officers," the soldier explained. *"Das ist standard protocol."*

"What?" the wife asked.

"You heard me," the soldier answered, as he tore the tickets in half and threw them under the train. "Now get your pretty little asses inside that first-class boxcar. *Schnell!*"

"We're not going in there," the wife said while crossing her arms over her broad chest. She was an imposing woman who always stood up for herself and her husband.

"Oh, no? Then you won't be going anywhere," the German soldier told her.

He took out his revolver, pointed it at the woman, and shot her between the eyes. He killed her husband the same way. The couple fell onto the platform.

Ben's body jerked suddenly, after hearing the loud gun shots.

"There. Your problem is solved, comrade," the young Nazi told the Hungarian soldier.

Four civilian men came onto the train platform, placed the dead couple into body bags, and they carried them away. The frightened crowd chaotically squeezed into the stinking boxcars. Some passengers only had room to stand. The doors were closed and locked, and the train sat in the station for two more hours while some mechanical repairs were made.

A rambunctious group of drunken German officers sang a patriotic song of the Fatherland as they joyfully meandered arm-in-arm along the station platform. They stumbled onto the train and noisily headed for the sleeping car.

A conductor handed the sinister-looking train engineer a steak sandwich and a small bottle of whiskey. The engineer thanked him and waved his dirty cap out the window. He blew his whistle, and the conductor announced the train would leave in two minutes. Some young soldiers boarded right before the doors were closed and the train sluggishly departed.

In the dining car, Captain Manheim ordered three more whiskeys. He shuffled a deck of cards, cut them, and then dealt. Sergeant Heimlich looked at his cards and cursed; he was quickly losing the money he had won from the captain's wager back at the brick factory. The corporal fared better, but not by much.

The soft orange glow of Budapest gradually faded, as the long iron horse disappeared into the black Slovakian countryside.

8

The morning sun climbed above the Austrian Alps, throwing glistening rays down its snow-capped heights. In a valley below the tall peaks, a serpentine river overflowed with schools of silver-speckled rainbow trout and healthy Danube salmon. The deportation train from Beregszász rolled past virgin forests, but the bucolic landscape appeared more like a blotched watercolor painting to the sleepless and hungover locomotive engineer; he dozed intermittently as the railroad tracks ebbed and flowed along the winding route. German high-ranking officers and soldiers just finished breakfast inside the stainless-steel dining car of the train, when the Vienna railway station came into focus. The groggy engineer pulled the brake lever, and the train wheels gradually rolled to a loud grinding stop. The obsequious little conductor yelled out, "Vienna Station. Vienna, Austria!"

The doors parted, and the soldiers and officers disembarked. A new engineer came on to start his shift while the old engineer staggered onto the station platform, where he was met by his irate wife, who hollered profanities at him; she slapped his head a couple times before they drove off in a dented BMW. The conductor announced the next destination before relaxing in the dining car, where he devoured an egg sandwich stacked with ham slices.

The train departed Vienna.

Ben listened while sporadic crying, then intervals of silence filled the cold boxcar. Air from the mountains had made it a little easier to breathe now. He held his bundle, pushed himself up, and struggled his way to the piss bucket. Reaching it, he just about died from the disturbing odor. Wall to wall bodies around him, Ben squeezed himself between some, and passed out.

Well into the Austrian countryside, the long train traveled past ancient castles, farms, and sleepy villages peppered with tall white church steeples and spires. A red-shingled roof of a Jesuit monastery appeared above a steep hill, and the train briefly stopped at a nutshell hamlet, where three Benedictine monks were met by a blue Mercedes that shuttled them to the cloistered abbey on top of the hill. The quiet river current of the Danube flowed nearby.

The train chugged another fifteen kilometers down the tracks until it coasted alongside a chalk-white building, the town of Mauthausen's train station. The fat conductor made his way through the sleeping cars, hollering: "Station Mauthausen! Wake up! Everyone off for Mauthausen."

Hung over, sleep-deprived, and penniless from the poker game they had the night before, Sergeant Heimlich and Corporal Wagner tiredly carried their duffel bags off the train while prison kapos with white armbands positioned wooden ramps against the boxcars. When the sergeant gave the order, soldiers unlatched the doors. And mean-spirited dogs tugged on their leashes and barked themselves into a frenzy, eagerly awaiting the fresh shipment of Jews and Gentiles recently deported from Hungary, Slovakia and Austria. Toward the rear of the train, boxcars painted with the large black capital *As* and *Ds*, remained locked; their human cargo was still sandwiched inside, groping for air.

After the designated boxcars were unloaded, Sergeant Heimlich and Corporal Wagner dropped their duffel bags into a waiting *Kübelwagen* before it drove off.

Ben wasn't sure if he was alive or not—not until the boxcar door opened and a harsh sunlight temporarily blinded him. A burst of life-giving oxygen flooded his lungs while someone's cold knees pressed against his back; he turned around and saw a dead man. Several others around him had also expired enroute. As if he was dreaming, Ben watched their etheric blue soul-bodies escape through their mouths, leave the boxcar, and fly up into the sky. The remaining orthodox Jews in the car recited the mourner's kaddish. The Jewish prayer for the dead.

German soldiers mechanically announced through white megaphones, "Everyone out. *Rouse!*"

Ben moved in excruciatingly painful increments; his neck, back, elbow, and knee joints cracked. He stood hunched-over. grabbed his compressed sack of clothes, and then carefully descended the ramp onto a concrete platform. He turned his stiff neck and caught sight of an exhausted but familiar face.

"Katz!"

The shoemaker recognized Ben's voice. He saw him waving by the car next to his. Mr. Katz raggedly approached him. They hugged.

"You're alive—thanks God—where are we?" Mr. Katz inquired.

"I don't know but the soldiers are speaking German."

"After riding in that death train, anywhere is good right now," Mr. Katz stated.

"I agree."

Ben and Mr. Katz heard someone's voice below them.

"We are in Austria," replied a Hungarian Gypsy dwarf who was no taller than the height of the men's waists. "The town is called Mauthausen. I used to come here when I worked for a traveling circus."

Ben looked down at the man. "Thank you, my friend."

"You're welcome, brother."

"Where's your wife?" Ben asked.

"Inside the boxcar. I couldn't move her. She wasn't breathing."

"Let's go back and take her out."

"I don't know if that's possible, Benjamin."

Just then, men dressed in prison clothes shouted, "Out of our way!" And they parked large push-wagons in front of the boxcars. The prisoners climbed into the wretched-smelling compartments and carried out the lifeless passengers one by one, loading them into the push-wagons before carting them away.

"There's my wife," Mr. Katz announced, as he noticed her on the top of some other bodies inside a push-wagon. "I will follow them to see if I can bury her," he said.

"Don't," Ben warned.

"Get back in line, Jew!" a soldier yelled, striking Mr. Katz's upper leg with a baton.

He cried out in pain.

"Be careful, Mr. Katz—there's nothing we can do about it now," Ben said.

"My poor Ruth," he lamented.

"I know. I wonder what happened to the rest of my family," Ben said.

"They were put into a boxcar toward the rear of the train. I wanted to go with them, but the soldiers refused."

Able to speak fluent German, Ben timidly asked a blond-haired soldier, "Pardon me."

"*Ja?*"

"Are we going to a labor camp?" Ben asked.

The soldier smiled and nudged a soldier beside him. "*Nein, tateleh.* There aren't any labor camps here. Only a concentration camp up the road."

"I don't know what that is," Ben stated.

The soldier explained, "A concentration camp is similar to a fine resort hotel. You'll enjoy a lovely private suite, a health spa, and a restaurant that serves three gourmet meals a day. The camp even has a tennis court, a golf course, and a heated swimming pool. You will have such a good time there—I envy you."

In between sucking on their cigarettes, both of the soldiers laughed. One of them made a sound from the back of his throat, and he spit a globule of mucus on the ground. Ben looked up at the soldier, knowing what he had told him could not be true.

"And where did you learn how to speak such proper German?" one of the soldiers asked Ben.

"At my school in Hungary. Will this be the last stop on the train line?"

"*Nein, tateleh,*" the soldier affectionately replied. "From here, the train will go on to other wonderful vacation resorts. Like Auschwitz, Dachau, Bergen-Belsen and Treblinka."

"Oh . . . *danke schön,*" Ben told the soldier.

"*Bitte schön, tateleh.*"

The two soldiers laughed again.

"Form a line and march!" another soldier screamed through a megaphone.

Ben, Mr. Katz, and the others unsteadily foot-slogged down the train platform and onto Mauthausen's main street. Women on their hands and knees fearfully glanced up at the new arrivals. A woman kapo shouted at them, and the female work crew resumed scrubbing the sidewalk with brushes and pails of soapy water.

"Keep marching!" a Hungarian kapo yelled to Ben's group. "Eyes front."

If the parade wasn't moving fast enough, soldiers and kapos hit them with sticks and wooden batons. The exiles trudged past several townsfolk appearing to be frozen-in-time. When the kapos or soldiers weren't looking, a few of the courageous and sympathetic locals dropped fruit, sandwiches, or lit cigarettes on the road for the men and women lucky enough to pick up.

The thousand or more exiles came to the outskirts of town, where they scaled a hill which led to a gravel drive. An imposing granite wall appeared. Above the entrance, the insignia of a large dark eagle and swastika was held in place with iron bars.

Before Ben and Mr. Katz passed through the prison's stone gate—they silently read a posted sign written in German: *Wilkommen zu Konzentrationslager Mauthausen.* Welcome to Mauthausen Concentration Camp.

9

Back at the Mauthausen train station, the fat little conductor hurriedly waddled alongside the same train that Ben and Mr. Katz had disembarked earlier. The conductor announced the next stop and clambered aboard. He sat in the dining room, drank an espresso, and then devoured the other half of his pastrami sandwich on pumpernickel bread.

At noon, the train departed the chalk-white station, leaving behind the group of Jewish women who were scrubbing the station platform on their hands and knees. The innocent little village of Mauthausen faded from view, as well as the pretty pink and blue wildflowers that swayed alongside the tracks. Now that many of the boxcars carried much less weight, the train moved faster. Three hours had gone by, and Captain Manheim carried his duffel bag off at a bustling Munich station. His wife and two young children warmly greeted him.

"Next stop, Dachau!" the conductor announced.

Men and women toasted and celebrated in the beer halls of Munich, as the deportation train passed through the city. A few kilometers later it arrived at a picturesque village known as Dachau. Not far down the tracks was a dreary place enclosed by barbed wire and ominous gray guard towers. The Dachau concentration camp appeared. The boxcars with the capital *Ds* were opened, and the wealthy and poor occupants stiffly climbed down from the freight containers and were escorted into the camp. The aged, crippled, and mothers with infants and young children were sent directly to the gas chambers. A select group of children were brought to a brick building, where doctors would perform cruel and bizarre medical experiments on them. Other groups of men, women, criminals, homosexuals, and political dissidents who were not taken to the gas chambers, were ordered to strip naked and place their tattered, or fashionable belongings into piles. Later recycled by camp prisoners. In separate groups, the naked men and women were lined up shoulder to shoulder against a backdrop of lofty pine trees. After what seemed like an eternity, the men in the firing squads held their rifles and awkwardly observed the undressed prisoners. While they waited for the orders to shoot, a few soldiers must have thought: *Do I not have a conscience? How will I live with this? I dare not tell my wife or children. I'm only following orders. If I refuse to kill them, I'll be charged with insubordination. I'm just following orders.*

While their lives flashed before their eyes, the naked women shielded their pubic areas and breasts. In the other group, blank-eyed men bashfully covered their privates. Some did not. The commands were given. And the firing squads pulled their triggers. Bullets flew through the pine-scented air. The victims fell. The soldiers turned their backs and left. A few minutes later, a group of striped prisoners loaded the naked men and women onto wagons and trucks, and they were hauled off to the crematory. Tractors and bulldozers plowed the remaining corpses into mass graves that were dug in a field behind the prisoners' barracks.

The train that originated from Beregszász left Dachau, traveled north, and soon crossed into German-occupied Poland, where it made its final stop at the infamous Auschwitz concentration camp. The tracks led the train a few meters from the camp's entrance. Polish and German soldiers wrenched open the boxcar doors, and with their bleak, frigid eyes, the dead and the living were greeted by a blinding sun and a cold summer air. Dressed in striped, ill-fitting prison uniforms, children stood behind a barbed-wire fence and watched, as the new shipment of exiles were unloaded. Moments later, another train pulled into the camp. And one after that. The freight trains arrived continuously day and night, transporting more Jews and Gentiles from Hungary. Other deportation trains came from big Polish cities like Warsaw and Krakow, or the impoverished Jewish shtetls in the bleak country landscapes of Poland, Ukraine, Czechoslovakia, Belarus, Lithuania, and Latvia.

Barely alive themselves, Mendel, Hanni, Herschel, and Raisel disembarked the train, tightly holding their bundles of belongings and wearily standing on the crowded Auschwitz train platform. Looks of hope, fear, shock and confusion covered their faces.

"I hope Ben is here, Mendel," Hanni said, nursing a bruise she received exiting the boxcar.

Mendel remained silent. He coughed into a soiled handkerchief and almost fainted when he inhaled a horrible odor.

"What's that smell, Papa?" Herschel asked.

"I don't know. Smoke from a factory maybe."

Herschel started to cry. Raisel comforted her brother by wrapping her arms around him. "It's all right, Herschel."

Polish soldiers and kapos ordered everyone to move along the train platform, join lines, and march.

Mendel and his family approached an iron gate with large German words welded onto an ornamental sign high above.

ARBEIT MACHT FREI

"What does that mean, Mendel?" Hanni asked while she pointed at the sign.

"It's German, for work will set you free."

"Oh?" Hanni asked again.

"*Igen*, sweetheart."

Dressed in white lab coats and gloves, male and female doctors examined the camp newcomers one by one. Hanni reached the front of her line, and a German doctor placed a stethoscope onto her chest and briefly listened to her strong but nervous heartbeat. The doctor grimaced and pointed her toward a group of crippled and elderly women, mothers with babies, and small children. The female doctor examined Raisel next. After asking her a few questions, the examiner quickly motioned her to join a group of healthy young women and older girls.

Mendel and Herschel stood at the front of their line. A tall male physician in a starched white lab coat marked something on a clipboard. The doctor focused his blue, wolf-like eyes on Mendel and son.

"How old are you?" the doctor interrogated.

"Forty-eight and a half," Mendel replied in German.

"Do a deep knee-bend for me," the doctor requested.

Mendel succeeded but struggled as he pushed himself up. He was dehydrated from the horrendous journey. The doctor gave him a disparaging glance while placing a stethoscope onto his chest. Mendel stared at a group of strong and healthy men nearby, hoping Ben might be with them. The doctor removed the medical instrument.

"Look at me," he sternly said. "Do you smoke cigarettes?"

"On occasion."

"Not a healthy habit."

"I know. My wife wants me to quit," Mr. Weiss stated.

"Don't worry—you will soon. You're not suitable for the work here. It will be too difficult for you," the doctor said in a sterile voice.

"But I can try . . . no?"

"*Nei!*" the doctor shouted in Polish. He ordered Mendel to join a large group of puny boys and elderly and crippled old men. One man sat crying in a wheelchair.

Herschel stepped forward next; his eyes sheepishly focused on the doctor's tall black boots. Avoiding his crooked smile.

"Is he your *fater*?" the doctor asked.

"*Ja,*" Herschel meekly replied.

"Age?"

"Eighteen."

"You look younger," the doctor said. "Make a fist and bend your arm."

He felt Herschel's weakened bicep muscle, and he told him to join the group his father was in.

After the selection process ended, male and female kapos led the groups to their next destination.

Inside a cold, damp building, female guards ordered Raisel and her group to remove their foul-smelling clothing. She took off her favorite dress, underwear, and the pair of red high heels Mr. Katz had made her. Except for their shoes, women inmates gathered the clothing into push wagons and burned it in piles in an empty field. Raisel and her group took freezing cold showers. After, the women and girls stood soaking wet on a concrete floor in a drafty room. They had no towels to dry their bodies. A few female prisoners sprayed the new group for lice. They were given scratchy gray prison uniforms and got dressed.

The new inmates sat on benches and skin-headed barbers cut their long and short locks. They shaved their heads bald. Afterward, Raisel and the other women and teenage girls were brought across the room and seated at a long table, where tattoo artists inscribed a blue, six-digit serial number onto each one's inner forearm; they were officially registered as prisoners of Auschwitz. Two female kapos brought Raisel and her group out into the septic air, where they were marched to a row of wood barracks.

Basking in the afternoon sunshine, two Nazi officers practiced hitting golf balls on a grassy field beyond a tall barbed-wire fence. Previously, a diesel-powered bulldozer had hollowed out a deep, rectangular pit in the field they played in. Dump trucks unloaded skin-and-bone corpses; a tractor pushed them into a wide grave and covered it with dirt. The tractor drove off while the powerful earth mover dug another hole. One of the German officers barked, "Fore!" as he swung a nine iron. The club made contact, and the ball soared high and fell into the gaping crater the earth mover had dug.

"Excellent shot, Klaus."

"*Danke.*"

"You know, Klaus, I'm eager to get back to Aachen. I really miss the golf course in my hometown. You must visit my family after we win the war. We'll play a proper eighteen holes, then have beers and thick juicy steaks in the backyard barbecue. How does that sound, Klaus?"

"I would enjoy that very much, Lieutenant."

"*Wunderbar.*"

The other officer placed his ball on a tee, swung his club, and then hit a line-drive shot that swerved downward and ricocheted off the departing bulldozer in the distance. The little ball swiftly rolled toward the large rectangular hole and dropped into the open mouth of a dead person.

"Nice swing, Gunther, but I would have to say that's interference. Why don't you try again."

On the other side of the tall barbed-wire fence, Hanni and the group she was in straggled along a dusty path. The afternoon sun glared down on them as Hanni lagged behind a few moments to admire some pretty iris flowers someone had planted for a border along the fence. She inhaled a ghastly smell while picking one of the flowers.

"Keep moving," a female Polish guard hollered.

Hanni's group of elderly women, mothers cradling babies, and young children, approached a long building where twelve chimney stacks billowed out a stinking white smoke. Ashes fell upon them as they hobbled to another building. On that one, the German word *duschraum,* was written above two metal doors. The kapos ordered the women and children to strip naked and form a line outside the building. They handed them chunks of soap and small boxes to deposit their jewelry, money, or eyeglasses.

In front of her, Hanni overheard two elderly women talk in Hungarian.

"This place frightens me, Ethel," Miriam, the shorter woman said.

"What are you so afraid of, sister?"

"Everything," Miriam answered. "Why did we have to come to Poland? We should have stayed in Budapest. It's freezing here."

"We had no choice," the bigger sister explained. "The Hungarian army would have killed us in Budapest."

"We could have hidden in the attic—I miss my cat, Ethel."

"She'll be fine. Mrs. Bonhoeffer said she'll take good care of her while we're away."

"We aren't going back to Hungary, sister. And I'll never see my cat again."

"Oh, please, don't talk like that, Miriam."

"Why? It's true. I wish we had wings so we could fly away from here. I don't want to take a shower, Ethel."

Hanni followed behind the two sisters, as they moved closer to the *duschraum* entrance.

"We'll smell like boar hogs if we don't wash ourselves, Miriam."

"I don't give a rat's ass. These Nazi bastards can go fuck themselves, as far as I'm concerned."

"Miriam, please . . . they will hear you."

Just then, one of the Hungarian kapos approached the line with a hard stick in her hand.

"Move along, ladies," the kapo urged. "Place your things in the box you received. They'll be returned to you later. After you clean yourselves, you'll get new clothes, and everyone will have coffee and cake in the dining room. Hurry up now."

An elderly woman asked while another kapo handed her a small chunk of soap, "Where are the towels and bathrobes?"

"Don't worry, grandma. I'll bring them to you. Go inside."

Before the two sisters in front of Hanni reached the shower room entrance, they moved off the line and whispered to each other.

The woman kapo approached the sisters, and she asked them in Hungarian, "Why aren't you going inside the shower room?"

Ethel, the taller woman, replied, "My sister doesn't feel well. If she isn't going in, I'm not either."

With a look of astonishment, the kapo exclaimed, "Both of you must take a shower. Go inside. Now!"

"I don't believe this is a shower room," the shorter sister adamantly said.

"Don't talk back!" the kapo shouted. The kapo raised her hard stick and whacked Miriam's frail arm. A red bruise appeared. "I said go in!"

"You hurt me."

Mirriam started crying, and the taller sister stepped between her and the kapo. The kapo raised her baton about to strike Ethel, when she grabbed it and walloped the kapo's jaw so hard, it fractured, leaving her semi-conscious on the ground a few moments.

"Don't you ever hit my sister again, you fat douche bag."

A female guard came over and asked the kapo holding her bloody mouth, "Why are you lying down? Get those prisoners inside the shower room. Rouse!"

"That woman hit me with my baton," the Hungarian kapo cried, pointing to the taller sister. "I think she broke my jaw."

After Hanni witnessed the brawl, she rapidly entered the *duschraum*. Moments later, she heard two gunshots fired outside. The group was packed into the bath house; its metal doors were slammed shut and locked from the outside. Desperate echoes reverberated inside the queasy blue chamber; an anemic yellow light bulb glowed from the ceiling. Hanni and the others stood under the showerheads and turned the faucets. No water came out.

From a small cubicle connected to the *duschraum*, a male guard looked through a glass peephole in a wall, and lecherously observed the naked and frightened women inside. As the guard espied the occupants, he casually smoked a cigarette. He opened the pressure on a valve, and a poison gas was let into the shower room. Inmates who were working outside heard the desperate screams within the *duschraum*. They turned their heads and kept working.

Mendel and Herschel entered the men's *duschraum*. It was also illuminated by an eerie yellow light on the ceiling. They could hardly move inside; the chamber was so crowded. Mendel took off his top hat and affectionately brushed the felt material before hanging it on a hook. Too ashamed to look at his father's nakedness, Herschel began to cry. His father comforted him by putting a hand on his son's trembling shoulder.

"I'm scared something terrible is going to happen to us, Papa," Herschel said.

"Me too, son. Me too."

No water came out of the shower heads there either.

A guard slowly released the poison Zyklon gas.

Mendel, Herschel, and the others felt a burning inside their nose, throat, and lungs.

One man pounded and kicked and scratched the locked metal doors, until his knuckles and feet became bruised and bloody.

Another man banged his head against the hard floor.

Others pulled their hair and screamed.

Mendel tightly held onto his son's arm and prayed.

The queasy blue walls spun around in a fiery circle.

Mendel felt as if his skin was burning from the inside out.

Everything stopped.

Silence filled the chamber.

The bodies lay still on the cold floor. Their souls escaped the gas chamber via the vent holes the poison gas had come through. Heavenly hosts met the rising spirits and helped them make their departure from the camp.

The *duschraum* doors were unlocked and opened. Two Hungarian kapos reluctantly peered inside, while a final glimmer of daylight peacefully landed onto the naked corpses.

10

June 1, 1944

Inside the Hungarian barracks at Mauthausen, a guard pointed his flashlight at Ben's face while a mean Lithuanian kapo bashed his hard stick against the prisoners' bedposts. Ben's eyelids snapped open like a sudden pull and release on a venetian blind. Mr. Katz awoke in the bed underneath. The guard and the kapo moved on to the next section of bunks.

"Rise and shine, scumbags!" the Polish guard yelled in Hungarian.

Ben sat up and quietly recited a Hebrew prayer said upon awakening: the *Modeh Ani*. "I offer thanks to You, my living God and eternal King, for You have mercifully restored my soul within me. Your faithfulness is great."

Ben and Mr. Katz climbed down from the bunk bed, and they put on their flimsy canvas shoes. The men used the primitive latrine inside the barracks. Afterward, they trudged to the communal washroom and splashed cold water onto their faces from a big round sink. Other prisoners elbowed for position behind the two men, while a sedentary dawn appeared from a large wood-framed window.

"Let's see what's on the breakfast menu, Ben," the shoemaker quipped as water dripped from his nose.

"Oh . . . sure."

Ben and Mr. Katz retrieved their metal bowls, cups, and utensils. They stood on a line and waited until the kitchen kapos served them a cold mush and a bitter tasting chicory coffee. They carried their breakfast to a long and crowded dining table, where several other Hungarian men sat.

Ben had barely swallowed two bites of slop when the mean Lithuanian kapo shouted, "Hurry up and finish eating, bastards! Wash up. Go outside for roll call. Now!"

A few men at the table laughed as Ben regurgitated his food after gunning down the muddy coffee. Everyone got up, washed their bowls, cups, and utensils, and then stored them in numbered lockers. The inmates gathered outside for roll call in the spacious garage yard.

While Ben waited for his name to be called, he closed his eyes a few moments, and his mother and father appeared in a vision. They rode on the horse-drawn wagon. A wreath of red roses adorned the horse's neck. The body of his younger brother, Herschel, rested inside a glass coffin on the wagon. Hanni and Mendel wore ghostly white shrouds except for his top hat and her yellow apron. Mendel gripped the reins and smiled at Ben. A mysterious purple light glowed around them, and their voices spoke through the foggy morning air:

Goal!

You want a ride home with us, Benjamin?

Give the horse an apple

Wash up for supper, Ben. How come you haven't milked the cow yet?

We're having stuffed cabbage tonight

Pearl wants to go to America, Mendel

And I suppose all the streets there are paved with gold?

Where is Newburgh, Hanni?

The vision suddenly disappeared. And Ben opened his eyes to the brackish morning sky. The disheveled prisoners around him coughed, cleared their throats, and spit.

A guard yelled, "Benjamin Veiss!"

"Present," he answered while waving his striped cap in the air.

"You're working in the quarry today," the guard shouted.

Ben nodded and covered his shaved head. He joined Mr. Katz, who stood in a work crew forming nearby. The guard called the next name on the roster.

"Applebaum!"

"Here."

Flanked by guards and kapos who were accompanied by vicious German shepherds and rottweilers, Ben and his work crew of almost a hundred left the garage yard and marched down the gravel road about a kilometer, until they saw the Wiener Graben rock quarry. At the far edge of the worksite, Ben smelled a fragrant odor coming from an evergreen forest nearby. Everyone stopped to urinate as the morning sun trickled over the forest behind the quarry. Huge white boulders and jagged rocks formed a stark terrain. Ben remained in the spot while the others sluggishly departed. He watched a flock of black kites and brown buzzards fly overhead. They called to him, speaking in a strange language he seemed to understand.

"You poor pathetic human being. How foolish of you to come here. We fly over this place daily, and watch hundreds perish from the hard labor. Mr. Weiss. You as well shall not survive this hell for very long."

Ben stood next to a tree and urinated. He suddenly realized that everyone had moved on toward the granite quarry. The birds circled the horizon once more and hovered above his head. Again, they spoke: "In the end, your oppressors will turn you into a walking skeleton, and when your body is put in the ground here, the worms will have little of you to eat."

One of the birds crapped on Ben's shoulder; he angrily stared up as the flock flew off.

"Hey! What are you doing over there, muscleman?" a guard yelled from a short distance away. He pointed a rifle with a sharp bayonet on the end of it. "Get moving, Jew. Or you'll be history."

Ben hurried to catch up with the others, passing a stagnant pond with a scummy green surface. The water appeared polluted.

He suddenly flashed back to what the Nazi soldier had told him when he arrived at Mauthausen. *"It even has a heated swimming pool, a tennis court, a golf course, and three gourmet meals a day"*. Ben brushed away the thought and caught up with his work detail. On the bottom of the quarry, at the base of a steep hill, a stone staircase had been built into a high mound. Another work crew was already climbing up the 186 rock steps to the top. Each laborer carried a heavy granite stone in a wooden carrier on their back. The multitude of men struggled like pack-mules up the perilous incline. Ben watched them from below.

"There you are—I've been looking for you," Mr. Katz told Ben. "Hurry up. Put on a carrier. I'll load your block. Then you can load mine."

Ben strapped on a wood-framed backpack, and Mr. Katz uneasily placed a heavy granite block inside. Ben lowered a block into his partner's carrier, and the bustling work crew soon started scaling the steps. At the top they followed a rutted road which led them to the Danube River. There, they loaded the granite stones onto long barges. Ben and the other prisoners made the long trudge back to the starting point at the bottom of the rock staircase. They replenished their carriers with granite, before starting the arduous routine all over again.

The midday sun scorched the labors in the quarry. Ben's work detail had decreased to about half. Many died from sunstroke, dehydration, injury and gunshot wounds. As a joke, guards with rifles would push prisoners off the top of the rock staircase. They would fall through the air, land on the granite floor below, and fatally fracture their skeletons. The guards would laugh.

By seven o'clock that day, the sun lowered beneath the stone horizon, and the kapos' loud calls reverberated inside the quarry.

"Work is finished! Everyone back to camp! Work is finished. Everyone back to camp. Work is finished. Everyone back to camp."

Ben took hold of Mr. Katz's arm and helped him hobble out of the quarry. They passed the stagnant pool, and onto the gravel road. When everyone reached the garage yard, they lined up for evening roll call. The dusky sky had turned a rotten mushroom blue black. The stars came out. Mr. Katz waited until Ben's name was called. Together, they limped back to Barracks 20.

"I'm dead tired, Benjamin. I don't know how I'll ever survive this work. Every muscle in my body hurts. I have terrible blisters on my feet."

"Mine too. We'll get some food soon. Then rest after."

"*Igen . . .*"

"Let's go," Ben said. "We're almost there."

Ben and Mr. Katz walked between several rows of long green buildings built from wood. They found Barracks 20, what they called home now. Dangling light bulbs shone through the barrack's spooky, white-framed windows. A brown door opened and closed as each dog-tired prisoner entered. The interior was furnished with numerous three-tiered sleeping bunks and long benches on either side of four long dining tables. By the entrance, two plain chairs were reserved for a guard and a kapo. A kitchen was located at the far end of the barracks. A communal latrine and a washroom supplied cold running water on the other side. Ben and Mr. Katz followed the other prisoners.

"Let's go to the latrine," Ben said. "Save a place next to you, if you get to the table before me."

"I will."

Mr. Katz went to his wooden locker and retrieved his metal bowl, cup, fork, and spoon. When he reached the front of the food line, a kitchen kapo plopped a tablespoon of rice into his bowl while another kapo ladled a watered-down soup into it. A haggard-looking potato peel floated on top. He was handed a clump of stone-hard black bread and found himself a seat at one of the long tables. He squeezed beside a lanky gentleman who wore tidy work clothes; his narrow face was clean-shaven, jet-black hair grown out and slicked back. Mr. Katz braved a taste of food.

"How is it?" Ben asked as he placed his tray on the table; he sat between the shoemaker and the lanky gentleman with the clean-shaven face.

"Nothing to write home about," Mr. Katz answered.

"Thanks to the almighty," Ben said. He lowered his head and closed his eyes a moment. He picked up the hard bread and knocked it against the table. It sounded as if a carpenter was hammering nails. The other men stopped chewing and looked up. They noticed Ben's sharp face and muscular upper body, a stark contrast to their gaunt frames.

Mr. Katz whispered, "Everyone's looking at us, Ben. Maybe you shouldn't knock your bread on the table like that."

"Oh." Ben cleared his throat and addressed the men, "Sorry if I disturbed you."

They acknowledged his apology with grunts and nods. One man smiled while the rest of them put their heads down and continued eating. The lanky man who sat next to Ben took hold of his hard portion of bread and banged it against the table. He teased the other diners with a dropped jaw and open mouth. A gold tooth shone in front. They burst out laughing. A few of them knocked their rolls against the table. And for the time being, the somber atmosphere in the barracks had been lifted. The lanky man nudged Ben's side with his elbow. He spoke to him in a city-like Hungarian:

"Put your bread in your soup, man. It will soften and be easier for you to eat."

"Oh, thanks . . ."

"You're welcome, brother."

Ben placed the bread in his bowl and spooned the warm yellowish liquid over it.

"My name is Zugreb. Zohar Zugreb," said the tall man with the slicked black hair.

"Benjamin Weiss. And this is my good friend and neighbor, Jacob Katz."

The men shook hands with their new friend.

"Pleasure meeting you both. You are new. Where do you come from?"

"Beregszász, Hungary," Ben replied. "Both of us."

"We are neighbors," Zohar stated. "My hometown is Budapest—have you been there?"

"I have."

"Never," Mr. Katz replied.

Ben ate a spoonful of soup, then paddled around the soaking bread.

"Where you working?" Zohar inquired.

"At the quarry," Ben replied. "Both of us."

"That's brutal work, my friend. Last week the guards pushed eight Dutchmen off the top of the quarry. They killed them all."

"Why?" Mr. Katz asked.

"Because they're cruel Nazis. What else? Maybe they weren't working hard enough. I liked the Dutchmen. I can speak their language. Nice group of people. Friendly. Educated. Decent men. Teachers, doctors, and lawyers. I doubt they were used to hard labor," Zohar said while he wiped away some tears.

"Oh," Ben said. "I'm sorry you lost your friends."

"Thank you. I know how difficult the work is at the quarry. I worked there the first two days I was here. I hated it. My third day, the commandant came to the barracks and asked if anyone knew how to do electrical work. I'm a master electrician, so I volunteered. I've been doing that work ever since, thank God. I would have been dead a long time, if I kept working at the quarry. Better you get jobs somewhere else."

"How long have you been in Mauthausen?" Ben inquired.

"Tomorrow will be my one-year anniversary. Do either of you have a trade?"

"I was an apprentice glazier in Hungary," Ben replied. "Almost a journeyman."

"Good. That's a very respectable trade," Zohar stated. "Not many men know how to cut glass. And what is your occupation, Mr. Katz?"

"Shoemaker, Mr. Zugreb."

"And he's an excellent one at that," Ben added.

"You should put those skills to work here," the electrician

spoke. "There's no glazier in the camp right now. I have to do some repairs in the guards' living quarters tomorrow. I'll tell the commandant's assistant I know someone who can fix broken windows."

"That's very kind of you," Ben said.

"Can you pull some strings for me?" Mr. Katz shyly asked the electrician.

Zohar finished his last spoonful of soup and tore off a piece of his softened bread. He turned to the shoemaker, "I'm sure there are plenty of Nazi boots around here that need repairing. I'll put in a good word for you also."

"I appreciate that, Mister Zugreb."

"Please. Call me Zohar. We are friends now."

"Are you Jewish?" Ben asked him.

"No, I'm a Protestant. The Nazis hate us too."

The Lithuanian kapo beat his long stick against the dining table. He yelled, "Supper time is over, cock suckers! Get your stinking asses out of here. Wash your plates. Go take showers. Now!"

"We have to leave," Zohar said. "Watch out for that kapo. He's a cruel son of a bitch. Don't trust him one minute. He would rat on his mother for an extra cigarette. Good night, gentlemen. We can talk tomorrow at supper. Save me a place by you at the table."

"We will. Good night, Zohar," Ben said.

Ben showered quickly and washed his filthy socks in the process. He let the sticky air dry him. He climbed up to a top bunk and hung his hand-washed socks from the bedpost, settling his exhausted body on a mattress of thinly layered straw.

"Did you get enough to eat, Benjamin?" Mr. Katz asked from the middle bunk.

"Yes, but I wish I had gone back for seconds. The roast beef and mashed potatoes looked delicious."

"Funny . . ."

A tiny bug gnawed at Ben's neck. "Something just bit me," he announced.

"You probably have lice," said the prisoner in the bottom bunk.

"Oh?" Ben asked.

"*Igen*. There's been an infestation of it recently," Ben's Hungarian neighbor replied. "If the fucking bastards don't delouse us more often—the creatures eat us up alive."

When another inmate heard the unsavory talk, he joined in, "Hey, muscleman. You know what we say around the camp?"

"What?" Ben asked.

"The lice here eat better than we do. Go to sleep. You won't feel them biting you as much."

The men laughed, and the Lithuanian kapo smashed his hard stick against Ben's bedpost. A guard hit a switch on the wall and the barracks turned pitch dark, aside for the guard's flashlight.

"Quiet! Lights out," the guard yelled.

Ben took his pocket watch from under the mattress; he gently placed it against his heart and felt the ticking. He slept.

11

The man in charge of Mauthausen, Commandant Graben, splashed through a puddle formed by an early morning sun-shower at the camp. Before he entered the officers' dining room, the five-foot nine-inch brown-haired and brown-eyed Austrian took a rag and wiped the water off his tall Nazi boots. He glanced at the sky and admired a broad and vibrant-colored rainbow. He went inside, poured himself a coffee, and then brought it over to his usual table by a window that had a pane missing. A woman approached the commandant's table. She wore a snug navy-blue V-neck sweater that complemented her grandiose breasts and red-freckled cleavage. She set her tray opposite the commandant.

"Pretty rainbow," the thirty-year-old curvaceous redhead remarked while gazing through the window.

"Indeed. Good morning, Mrs. Holstein," the commandant greeted his secretary while wiping some cream off his square brown mustache.

"You're not eating breakfast?" she asked.

"Don't have an appetite—my ulcers are bothering me this morning."

"Sorry to hear," Mrs. Holstein said as the commandant enviously eyed the flirtatious woman's eggs Benedict, rye toast, hash browns, four strips of bacon cooked crisp, and two sausage links.

"See you're eating a healthy breakfast this morning," he stated.

"I'm skipping lunch today," she said, draping a cloth napkin across her pleated black skirt; she wore no panties underneath it. A gaudy pair of fourteen-karat gold earrings dangled from her earlobes. They were a birthday present given to her by an admiring guard at the camp; the jewelry once belonged to a Jewish countess from Romania, who'd been stripped of it before dying in the gas chamber at Hartheim Castle.

The secretary bit into her toast while the commandant secretly observed the hollow between her breasts. Her aqua-blue eyes shimmered in the morning light. The tall German formed an erection under the table as his secretary smiled at him, had a bite of sausage, and then generously salted and attacked one of her eggs.

Corporal Wagner opened the door to the dining room, letting in a late spring breeze. The imprudent Mrs. Holstein felt the draft waft between her pale, fleshy thighs. She crossed her legs. The corporal closed the door then glanced at the red headed woman at the table by the broken window. The corporal poured a cup of coffee and took a bowl and filled it with oatmeal from the steaming hot buffet table. His vision blurred some as his coke-bottle eyeglasses fogged up a few moments.

"How's your mother doing these days?" the secretary asked the commandant.

"She's well, thanks. Somewhat bored in Berlin. She's unable to get out much, since the bombing started. I'm planning a visit in a month or so . . . depending how the war goes."

"Is she safe in Berlin?"

"There's a bomb shelter in the basement of her building."

"That's good."

"Well, I won't get much work done if I stay around here," the commandant said. "That reminds me, Mrs. Holstein. I'd like you to type a letter today," he said while giving her a paper with writing on it. "It's for my mother. She has a difficult time reading my handwriting."

"I know," the secretary said, grinning. She salted and forked her other egg.

Corporal Wagner greeted them at the table. "Good morning, Commandant. Mrs. Holstein. Mind if I join you?"

"Morning, Corporal," the commandant said, detecting an offensive odor coming from the other man's direction. "I see you're back from Hungary. I'm leaving but I'm sure that Mrs. Holstein would enjoy your company."

The commandant took his briefcase and left the table.

*Don't be so sure of that, Commandan*t, the woman thought, as she caught a whiff of the corporal's overripe body odor. The secretary gave the young corporal an uninterested stare. She uncrossed her stockingless legs and pushed away her half-eaten breakfast. She removed a cigarette and a lighter from her fashionable Parisian handbag while the corporal sat beside her. She lit the cigarette and blew the smoke past his pudgy red nose.

"It's good to see you again, Mrs. Holstein," the corporal said. "How are you?"

"I'm fine. But you need a bath. You *shtink*."

"I'm sorry. I had a long train ride. I'll get one after I eat."

"Please do," the secretary said, as she got up from the table and quickly squashed her cigarette in an ash tray. "Have a good day, Mr. Wagner."

"*Danke . . .* you as well, Mrs. Holstein."

On his way to the administration building, the commandant pulled out a dandelion weed that was growing along the sidewalk. He stashed the yellow flower inside his shirt pocket, opened a door, and then marched down a hallway that was littered with portraits of himself, Führer Klaus Von Hellmenz and other bigwigs in the Nazi party. He paused to straighten one of the frames before going inside his office. He set his briefcase on a desk and opened the venetian blinds; a ray of light landed on an oak shelf, where two potted philodendrons and a fish aquarium sat. He fed the fish, watered the plants, and then heard a knock on the door.

"Come in."

Sergeant Heimlich opened the door and greeted his superior officer with an arm raised high in a starched Nazi salute.

"Heil Hellmenz, Commandant."

Graben wrinkled his nose as if he had just smelled a dead rat inside the room.

"Ya . . . heil Hellmenz, Heimlich. What the fuck? Lower your arm already. You haven't bathed this morning?"

"*Nein.* I just came from the train station. And I ran out of cologne while I was in Hungary. Not to mention, the hotel we were staying at only had freezing cold water."

"That's unfortunate. So how was your trip, sweetheart?" the commandant asked his lover.

"Exhausting—but productive."

"I presume the deportation proceedings went well?" the commandant asked.

"Like clockwork. Would you like to hear the statistics?"

"Please," the commandant replied as he reached into his pocket and gently pulled out the dandelion he had picked earlier. He inserted it into a small vase filled with water. He sat at his desk and lit a cigarette.

The blond and blue-eyed Austrian unfolded a paper and read from it:

"Two transport trains delivered twelve hundred Hungarian Jews, sixty-five Gypsies, fifty-two Jehovah's Witnesses, twelve Seventh-Day Adventists, thirty Russian officers, five American airmen, eleven Canadian airmen, fifteen British soldiers, eighteen Negroes, sixteen homosexuals, twenty non-Jewish political dissidents, a large family of midgets, and twenty-five young and attractive Hungarian women for the brothel. Wealthy ladies from Budapest."

The sergeant folded the paper, stood there, and proudly gloated.

"Excellent job, Heimlich."

"Danke schön."

"Work them until they're skin and bones. And send the sick and crippled straight to the gas chambers."

"Jawohl, Commandant."

"It's been rather lonely around here without you," the brown-haired commandant said to the handsome, blue-eyed, flaxen-haired Aryan man.

"I missed you too."

"Did you get a haircut?" the commandant inquired.

"A Jew hairdresser gave me one in Beregszász."

"Brings out your pretty blue eyes. She made a good job."

"He made a good job. The barber was a man."

"A man? You were with someone else in Hungary, hey, Heimlich?"

"Of course not. He only gave me a haircut and a shave."

"Are you sure that's all the Jew barber gave you?"

"Yes, Commandant. Are we finished with the interrogation?"

"I feel like you're not being entirely honest with me, Sergeant."

"Oh, please, spare me the melodrama."

"I was only joking. Lighten up, sweetheart."

The commandant picked up a heavy glass paperweight on his desk. He shook the object, then watched as tiny snowflakes fell onto a miniature Christmas tree. A Santa Claus waved from inside the paperweight. It was a gift from his mother last year.

"Oh—I almost forgot," the sergeant said. "Mrs. Holstein gave me a telegram for you. The Headquarters of the High Command in Berlin sent it a few minutes ago. It's marked extremely important."

"Read it."

The sergeant sat on a chair and unfolded the telegram.

"Sent at 9:00 a.m. June 2, 1944. Official business. To Commandant Graben. Mauthausen Concentration Camp. On July 4th, at exactly three o'clock in the afternoon, Major Wolfgang Himmel, Lieutenant Karl Flügel, and Captain Herman P. Segan will arrive in Mauthausen to make an official visit and inspection of the camp's facility. The officers' wives will accompany them. You will prepare accommodations and meals for the entourage of six guests, two soldiers, and one chauffeur. They'll be staying at your private villa for two days and two nights. Be sure to make all the necessary preparations.

Sincerely Yours,
Mrs. Helga T. Glockenshpiel
Secretary to Führer Klaus Von Hellmenz
Office of the SS High Command in Berlin"

"Let me see that," the commandant said.

The sergeant handed him the telegram.

"That's awfully odd," the commandant stated while noting the official seal of the SS High Command stamped on the top of the telegram. "I wonder why Berlin didn't give me more notice about this matter."

"I'm sure the Führer has his reasons," the sergeant said.

"Suppose you're right. You'll have to organize a proper welcoming reception for the visitors. Inform the steward and the head chef immediately. We must have the finest food, champagne, and wine. Call your friend, Prior Mueller at the monastery. And see if he can procure some of that Benedictine and Brandy they make there. Get an extra case of wine also. No skimping. Understood, Heimlich?"

"Ja, of course."

"*Wunderbar*. Has the electric fence been repaired yet?" the commandant questioned.

"Prisoner Zugreb said it was done this morning. By the way, the electrician knows a couple of new prisoners who have valuable work skills."

"What kind of skills?"

"One's a shoemaker," the sergeant replied. "The other man is a glazier. I met the glazier and his family when we were in Hungary."

"Where are they working now?"

"At the quarry."

"Have the two prisoners in my office this afternoon," the commandant said. "And I want you go to town and have our dress uniforms cleaned and pressed. Take a hot bath first."

"Anything else while I'm in town?"

"Yes, sweetheart," the commandant replied. "Why don't you get us a few bottles of that dark beer I like. And two fat ham sandwiches on pumpernickel. Extra mustard on mine. And do me a huge favor while you're in town?"

"What's that?"

"Get yourself a nice bottle of cologne. And one for Corporal Wagner. Put everything on the Mauthausen account."

"*Ja.*"

"And one more thing . . ."

The sergeant looked back from the open doorway.

"*Ja?*"

"Don't forget the half-sour pickles."

12

In the late afternoon, a Kübelwagen transported Ben and Mr. Katz from the quarry back to the camp and brought directly to the administration building. They stood in the commandant's office; their camp uniforms still covered with a fine white dust from work. Their faces, arms and necks well sunburned.

The commandant leisurely finished the other half of his ham sandwich and wiped some mustard off his square brown mustache. He turned up his nose, and inspected the yellow Jewish stars sewn onto the men's shirts.

"My name is Commandant Graben, and this is my faithful assistant, Sergeant Heimlich. I was informed that one of our trusted electricians recommended both of you." The commandant admired Ben's strong physique a moment. "What's your name, muscleman?"

"Benjamin Weiss."

"What type of work do you do, Weiss?" the commandant asked.

"I'm a glazier."

"You can fix windows?"

"Ja."

"Do you cut glass?"

"Ja."

"Are you skilled at it?"

"I'm not a master glazier—almost a journeyman."

"That should do," the commandant said, as he took a hand-brush and cleaned the dust from Ben's yellow Jewish star. "But if you don't do a good job, you'll hang from the gallows. Is that clear? Prisoner Weiss.

"Ja."

"Gut. Tomorrow morning, I want you to install three mirrors inside the guest rooms at my private villa. A window at the officers' dining room needs to be repaired also. Go with the sergeant. He will show you where your tools are located."

"*Danke shoen*," Ben said.

Ben and the sergeant left the office, while Mr. Katz waited for his interrogation, nervously cracking his knuckles. The commandant stood at his desk and opened a gold-plated cigarette box. He removed two cigarettes.

"Cigarette?"

"No, thank you. I don't smoke."

"Where are you from?"

"Beregszász, Hungary."

"What's your name, Jew?"

"Jacob Katz."

"The shoemaker, I presume?"

"I'm sorry, my German isn't so good."

"I can speak Hungarian if you'd prefer. How long have you been a shoemaker?"

"Twenty-five years."

"I want you to make me a pair of black dress boots. With a zipper on the side. Can you do that?"

"If you provide me with the shoe leather and—"

The commandant interrupted, "Your tools and materials will be at your new workbench in the maintenance building. We'll go there shortly. I want the boots in six days. If not—you'll go back to work at the quarry—understand, Katz?"

"Igen, Commandant."

"Measure my feet," the commandant said, while he tossed Mr. Katz a cloth measuring tape. He sat down and placed his legs up onto his desk. "Take off my boots."

Ben and the sergeant walked through the garage yard and into the camp's maintenance building. Various tradesmen momentarily looked up from their workbenches as the two men went over to a square table covered with a thin rug. The sergeant pulled a chain that illuminated a single light bulb above the table.

"Is it coincidence, or destiny we meet again, Mr. Weiss?" the sergeant asked.

"That's a good question, Sergeant. Do you happen to know where the rest of my family went?"

"If they aren't here, they were probably taken to Auschwitz or Dachau maybe. This is your work area, Weiss. You have all your tools, glass, and mirror of various measurements. Can you think of anything else you might need for the job?"

"A glass cutter mighty come in handy," Ben replied.

"Yes, I have them right here," the sergeant said, as he pulled a small cardboard box from his shirt pocket. It contained two brand-new diamond-blade glass cutters. "Don't lose them. They were expensive. You'll be responsible for keeping all the tools secure. If they get stolen or lost—you'll be punished. Here's the key for your tool locker. Lock it at the end of your shift. You'll work six days a week. Monday through Saturday. In exchange for the work, you'll receive camp money to purchase various goods at the prison commissary. The money can also be used to pay for the services of a young woman in the camp's brothel. Unless you happen to be a homosexual. In which case you would have to make other arrangements," the sergeant explained with an unchaste grin.

"I'm not a homosexual, Sergeant."

"Regardless. This is your work pass. It will allow you to go unaccompanied anywhere in the camp. All you have to do is show it to the guards or kapos."

The sergeant gave Ben a small yellow document with his name hand-printed and the sergeant's signature below it.

"I want your work area thoroughly cleaned and organized. Then you'll go to the administration building, and the commandant's secretary will validate your work pass. When you enter the building, go down the hall; her office is the first door on the left. It's imperative you address her as Mrs. Holstein. She's right next to the office you were in this afternoon. Meet me here tomorrow morning. Six-thirty sharp. Don't be late, or I'll dock you a whole day's pay. Do you have any more questions, Weiss?"

"*Ja.* What is Auschwitz or Dachau?"

"Death camps," the sergeant bluntly stated.

"Oh."

After Ben swept and organized his work area, he shut off the light above his worktable and headed for the administration building. Inside, he passed the portraits in the hall, and knocked on Mrs. Holstein's door. Her stern voice loudly called from within.

"Enter."

Ben opened the door and awkwardly stood with the yellow work pass in his hand.

"What do you want, Jew?" the secretary snapped.

"Sorry to disturb you, Mrs. Holstein. Sergeant Heimlich sent me here to have my work pass validated."

The redhead folded a letter and placed it inside a white envelope. She licked an Austrian postage stamp that displayed the führer's dog-bitten face and stuck it on the envelope. She glanced at Ben.

"Come in, Jew. Close the door."

He shut it and slowly approached Mrs. Holstein's desk as she sprayed herself with a floral perfume. She lifted the hem on her skirt and displayed her pale upper thighs. She bent over and pulled open a bottom drawer. Searching through it, she freely exposed her cleavage. Ben's eyes widened a bit.

"Where is that damn thing!" She looked up. "What are you looking at, Jew?"

"Nothing," he said, rapidly diverting his eyes to the wall.

"Don't lie, I can tell you were looking at me. You find me attractive?"

Ben thought for a moment.

"Oh."

"Oh, what?" she asked.

"You are attractive, Mrs. Holstein."

"*Danke schön.* If you'd said anything less, I would have sent you to the gas chambers. Give me that work pass."

He handed her the yellow document.

"My validation stamper must be in the commandant's office. Follow me," she said, picking up the stamped envelope.

They walked to the office next door.

"Wait outside," she ordered.

The secretary cracked open the door without knocking. She quietly entered. "Commandant, I finished typing your mother's letter. Would you like to read it? And I need to validate a prisoner's work pass—have you seen the stamper?"

The secretary covered her mouth in surprise.

"I put it on your shelf this morning," the commandant snapped in reply, "Get out of here!"

Mrs. Holstein dropped the envelope on the floor at the sight of the commandant's bare white ass. His pants had been pulled down to the top of his boots. A hand that wasn't his own, clutched him from behind his hip.

"I said—get out!"

That evening, back in Barracks 20 at the supper table, Zohar squeezed between Ben and Mr. Katz: he set down his ration of hard bread and watery soup, then briefly bowed his head and prayed. He raised his head and smiled. "Good evening, gentlemen. Pass the salt, please."

"Good evening, Zohar," Ben returned the greeting while reaching for a metal shaker with holes in the top. "We'd like to thank you for getting us our new work assignments, Zohar."

"You're welcome—are your workbenches in the maintenance building?"

"*Igen.*"

"Mine is there also," Zohar stated. "By the way . . . the commandant is throwing a big party at his villa in a few days. I've worked his parties before. It's an easy job. And he pays well.

He'll need two extra men to help out in the kitchen and dining room. You'll have plenty of delicious food to eat. Not like this shit. Either of you interested?"

"I'm in," Ben answered.

"Me too," Mr. Katz added.

"Good. I'll inform Sergeant Heimlich tomorrow morning."

13

Bells rang out through the halls of an elementary school in the village of Mauthausen, signaling the end of school that day, and the official start of summer vacation. A teacher, Mrs. Eichholtz, erased the history lesson on the chalkboard while three fifth-grade boys grabbed their book bags and lunch boxes and dashed out of the room before anyone else. Hans, Peter, and Adolf cut through a neatly landscaped school yard, went through a green gate, and then happily walked to the neighborhood where they lived.

"Now that summer vacation is here—we'll be able to enlist in the Nazi youth brigade," said the flaxen-haired boy named Adolf.

"*Ja,* Adolf. I'm really excited about it," Hans mentioned, as his blue eyes widened. "A cousin of mine who lives in Frankfurt said his unit gets to shoot live ammunition sometimes."

"What do they shoot, Hans?" Peter inquired.

"They shoot Jews—of course."

Adolf laughed as he bent down to tie his shoelaces. "Do you think your cousin is telling the truth, Hans?"

"I don't know. Why?"

"Just wondering," the flaxen-haired youth answered while four giggling schoolgirls passed by them. Their long pigtails swayed from side to side.

"Shall we play by the camp today, boys?" Peter asked. "Maybe we'll see something exciting."

"*Ja.* We'll meet at my house this time," Adolf replied. "And don't forget to bring your binoculars, Hans."

The three schoolboys returned to their homes, changed into play clothes, and then wolfed down milk and cookies. Hans and Peter kissed their mothers goodbye. And they ran over to their friend's house and rang his doorbell.

"Hello, Mrs. Eichmann," the two youths greeted.

"Hello, boys, Adolf will be right out," a woman greeted. Her golden-haired son grabbed his army canteen and came outside.

"See you later, *mutter,*" he told his mother, and kissed her on the cheek before running off to play.

"Don't be late for supper, Adolf. I'm making schnitzel tonight."

"*Nein, mutter,*" he called back.

A cat rubbed against Mrs. Eichmann's leg as she smiled and watered her multicolored pansies beside the porch.

Hans, Peter, and Adolf followed some railroad tracks by their neighborhood, until they came to a gravel road, leading them to the Mauthausen concentration camp. The youths climbed a tall oak tree planted on the other side of an electric barbed wire fence, their favorite spot. From the lofty perspective they clearly observed hundreds of naked inmates inside the spacious garage yard.

"That's disgusting," Hans remarked. "The men aren't wearing any clothes."

"The guards are spraying something on them," Adolf said.

"That's to get rid of their lice," Peter stated. "My father told me. He delivers milk to the camp twice a week."

"Does he?" Hans inquired.

"Ja."

In a more distant view emaciated prisoners appeared almost ant-like in size. They were climbing the staircase of death inside the Wiener Graben rock quarry. Hans peered through his binoculars and observed several prisoners who were standing atop the quarry stairs. Guards stood behind them and pushed the prisoners off the cliff with the ends of their rifles. The men flew off and landed on the hard quarry floor—alive for only a few moments.

"Oh, my God, that's terrible," Hans said.

"Let me have a look, Hans," Adolf requested as he reached for his friend's binoculars.

"Here—be careful—it's not a pretty sight."

Peter braced himself against an oak limb, and he checked the time on his wristwatch. It was three o'clock on the dot. The youth curiously watched as a *Kübelwagen* and a glossy blue Mercedes drove up to the camp's guard gate and stopped.

Peter pointed, "Look how shiny that car is, boys!"

The other two took notice.

"*Hei!*" Adolf exclaimed in German. "That is shiny. It must be a brand-new car."

"Impressive," Hans stated.

The sentry at the guard gate raised his arm.

"Heil Hellmenz," greeted the soldiers inside the Kübelwagen.

"Heil Hellmenz," Corporal Wagner said, squinting through his coke-bottle lenses. "What is the purpose of your visit to Mauthausen?"

"We're from the High Command in Berlin," replied one of the soldiers. "The high-ranking officers and their wives are behind us."

"You're clear to pass—park by the Kübelwagen—someone will meet you there shortly," the corporal said.

The corporal raised the wooden bar at the front gate, and the ultra-blue Mercedes and the lackluster gray military vehicle drove inside the camp. They parked, and the driver of the blue Mercedes helped the officers' wives out of the limo while their husbands lingered inside a few minutes.

The three women chatted with each other, taking little interest in Mauthausen's vulgar granite facade. They wore identical mink stoles over red satin blouses, white gloves, pleated black skirts, stockings with garter belts, polished red heels, and pretentious black hats with hanging white tassels. One woman opened her umbrella and shielded herself from the bright sunlight. Another woman checked her heavily made-up face in a compact mirror, while the third woman casually smoked from a gold-plated cigarette holder. They watched as a guard relentlessly beat a prisoner chained to a stone wall nearby. The poor man displayed an inverted pink triangle on his bloodstained shirt, identifying him as a homosexual. The prisoner screamed for mercy, and the women turned their gazes away from the brutal spectacle. One of them spoke as she opened a silk hand-fan painted with Japanese flowers.

"Why must there be such a flagrant display of cruelty right here at the front entrance?"

"I don't know, Greta," replied the woman who looked at her face in the compact mirror. "It's rather barbaric, if you want my opinion."

"I must agree. It certainly doesn't leave me with a good impression of the place."

"I have to pee soon," said the woman under the shade umbrella.

"Me too," Greta said.

"Perhaps we should wait till we get somewhere more civilized," said the woman fanning herself. "I don't suggest we use the facilities inside the camp."

"I hope that won't be too long, girls, or I just might wet my undies," Greta, the major's wife, joked.

The women cackled while their husbands climbed out of the car and donned their military caps. The three high-ranking officers focused on the tall oak tree on the other side of the electric fence. They waved to the boys who were perched high up in the tree. The youths held onto their branches and waved back. A pride welled up in them, seeing the officers' handsome military uniforms that were decorated with gold and silver medallions. The next moment, the boys watched as the three officers suddenly turned into angels. Each had a set of wings: one a bright crimson red; another a dazzling gold; and the third, a lustrous blue, like the paint on the Mercedes. The youths felt a loving warmth wash over their bodies. The angels' faces glowed as if they were on fire.

"Hans, Adolf! Do you see what I see?" Peter nervously inquired.

"Yes, we do," the other two boys replied in unison.

Hans accidentally dropped his binoculars, landing on the hard ground below. The youths were awestruck. The celestial beings turned back into high-ranking officers, and the three boys hurriedly climbed down from the tall, majestic oak. Hans retrieved his binoculars, and they quickly left their fantastic playground behind. The boys ran until they stopped to catch their breaths. Adolf drank from his water canteen. They gazed into each other's excited eyes. Hans examined his field glasses.

"Are they broken?" Peter asked.

"Strange . . . not even a scratch," Hans replied. "We must have been dreaming before."

"It was real, Hans," Peter said. "I saw them with my own eyes."

"I did too," Adolf said.

"We must promise never to tell a soul about what we saw back there," Hans mentioned. "Not even our mothers or fathers."

"They wouldn't believe us anyway," Adolf stated.

"*Nein.* If we tell anyone, we'll be locked up in the insane asylum," Peter said.

"I agree," Adolf added. "At Hartheim Castle. That's where the Nazis are gassing Jews—and the mentally ill."

"*Ja.* This will be our secret," Hans said.

Peter glanced at the time on his wristwatch. "Gosh . . . let's go, boys—we'll be late for supper."

Hans, Peter, and Adolf were greatly changed after what they had experienced that day. And they vowed never to join the Nazi Youth Movement, nor enlist in the military, nor go anywhere near the concentration camp ever again.

Back at the camp, the high-ranking officers turned from the tall oak tree and observed the hilly landscape in the opposite direction.

"There's nothing like the sweet innocence of youth," Major Himmel mentioned to his colleagues.

"I agree," Captain Segan said, as he picked a picked bright red feather off his sleeve.

The major looked through his binoculars and saw an old terracotta building with two wooden crosses on the roof. He lowered the field glasses and pointed his finger. "That might be a monastery over there," he mentioned. "I heard there was one close by."

"Let me have a look?" the lieutenant asked his superior officer.

Meanwhile, Sergeant Heimlich kicked up a small cloud of gravel as he marched over to greet the three dignitaries and their wives. The sergeant was startled by the lustrous blue car in the background.

"Heil Hellmenz, officers, ladies. My name is Sergeant Heimlich. Welcome to Mauthausen."

"Heil Hellmenz, Sergeant," the major greeted. "Sergeant, I'm Major Wolfgang Himmel, and this is my wife, Greta. Lieutenant Karl Flügel, his lovely wife, Hannah. And this is Captain Herman P. Segan, and his dear wife, Maria."

"I'm extremely pleased to meet you all," the sergeant said.

"We've heard a lot about you back in Berlin," the major mentioned, releasing his firm grip on the sergeant's hand.

"You have?" the sergeant asked, confused, as he felt a strange energy circulate inside his chest.

"Of course," the major replied. "We know more than you would believe, Sergeant."

"Everyone will be staying at the guest quarters in the commandant's private villa," the sergeant announced. "Cocktails and hors d'oeuvres are scheduled two hours from now. We'll have a lovely dinner afterwards."

"Wunderbar, Sergeant. Where is the commandant's villa located?" the major inquired.

"Not far from here. Have your soldiers and chauffeur follow me."

"I don't mind riding with you," the major said.

"You're most welcome, Major, but I'm certain my Kübelwagen isn't as comfortable as your Mercedes."

"I like to rough it sometimes," the major said, turning toward the sergeant's drab gray army vehicle.

The three women and the other two officers got back inside the blue limo, and the driver and their military escort followed the sergeant's Kübelwagen out of the camp, then onto a well-paved road for about a kilometer. The three vehicles climbed a steep hill and up a long driveway; at the top, a secluded villa appeared. From a bedroom window on the second floor, Commandant Graben espied the shiny blue Mercedes. He snorted another line of cocaine while his butler turned a gold-plated faucet in the bathroom, filling a brass-footed tub with hot water and liquid to make a lavender-scented bubble bath.

The sergeant parked the Kübelwagen, and he quickly opened the door for the major.

"This is it," he announced.

"Gorgeous property," the major remarked.

"It's beautiful up here," the major's wife mentioned. She admired some scarlet begonias bordering a white flagstone walkway. Bougainvillea plants hung along a wrap-around porch.

"Peaceful," Lieutenant Flügel's wife said to her husband.

"*Ja . . .*"

The sergeant escorted everyone to a side entrance of the villa. Two foot soldiers followed the entourage from behind, carrying the guests' luggage and their garment bags inside.

"These are the guest rooms you'll be staying in," the sergeant announced. "Each one has a private bathroom. Major, you and your wife will have the largest room at the end of the hall. There's a heated whirlpool tub on the deck outside. You'll find it most relaxing for tired muscles."

"Wunderbar," the major said, while his wife and the other two women quickly proceeded to the guest room down the hall.

"This is your room, Lieutenant," the sergeant announced.

"It's beautiful marble tile," he remarked about the polished white floor.

"That's not marble, Lieutenant," the sergeant stated. "It's polished granite."

"And why so much of it?"

The sergeant smirked and nonchalantly replied, "The cheap cost of labor and materials."

"The commandant must have a good friend in the construction business," Major Himmel said.

"The camp prisoners built the villa, Major," the sergeant stated. "The stone for the walkways, floors, kitchen counters, and bathroom vanities all came from the granite quarry near the camp. It didn't cost us one pfennig. Well . . . the workers received a minimal wage. Those who were fortunate enough to survive the construction project."

"I see," Major Himmel said.

"Our butler will come for you in two hours," the sergeant informed the major. "Make yourselves at home. I'll show your soldiers and driver where their sleeping quarters will be."

Meanwhile, in the most spacious guest room down the hall, the officers' wives made light conversation with each other. Hannah Flügel glanced at a portrait of Führer Hellmenz above a large brass bed. "There he is again," she said, lifting her feathery brown eyebrows.

"*Ja* . . . it's as if we can't get away from him," Greta Himmel stated. She kicked off her red high heels.

"Seriously," Mrs. Flügel critiqued. "He's not a very attractive looking man, is he?"

"*Nein*," Mrs. Segan said. "He ought to do something about that pathetic-looking mustache for heaven's sake. Looks like he stuck some dog shit under his nose."

The women exploded into a boisterous laughter. Moments later, their husbands walked into the room, interrupting the jovial atmosphere.

"I'm sorry I missed the punch line, Greta," the major said. "What's so funny?"

"We were just having a little girl talk."

"Come, Hannah . . . we'll take a nap before we meet the commandant," the lieutenant said, nudging his wife's arm.

"You as well, Maria," Captain Segan said to his spouse.

The two couples left the guest room, and Greta finally got to go to the bathroom. The major stood in front of a window that looked out onto a redwood deck, where the whirlpool tub sat. *We'll have to take a soak tonight,* he thought, as he closed the drapes. He unbuttoned his white shirt, unbuckled his belt, unzipped his pants, and then tiredly plopped onto an armchair, where he pulled off his well-worn yet polished Nazi boots. He combed a hand through his thick growth of silvery-blue chest hair, noticing the portrait of Führer Hellmenz over the bed. The major pulled up his nose and held a silver crucifix that was around his neck. He made the sign of the cross.

"Greta?"

"Yes, darling?"

"Will you be having a bath before we meet the commandant?"

"I will . . . why?" she asked, brushing her voluminous blond hair in the bathroom mirror.

The major remained silent.

His wife came into the room dressed only in her stockings, garter belts, and white silk panties. She stood topless in front of her husband—with the most broad and brilliant blue wings—an angel could ever have.

"What were you saying, darling?" she asked.

14

Crystal chandeliers and shimmering candlelight illuminated the living room at the villa on top of the hill. The three high-ranking officers and their wives made their grand entrance to the gala hosted by Commandant Graben and Sergeant Heimlich. The three women wore elegant silk evening gowns; gold, silver, and sparkling diamond jewelry beautified their necks, earlobes, wrists and hands. Their husbands were handsomely attired in jet-black, formal military uniforms and high dress boots. White carnations decorated their lapels. Welcoming the guests, a classical pianist in a tux, one wild-haired, long-nosed prisoner from the camp, sat next to a baby grand piano and deftly performed a nocturne composed by Chopin. Zohar Zugreb loomed behind the bar in the living room, cordially smiling at the guests. The lanky Hungarian from Budapest was decked in a pair of tuxedo pants, starched white shirt and vest, silk bow tie and shiny black shoes; he was the official barman of the evening.

The wild-haired piano player was startled when Zohar popped the cork from a bottle of expensive champagne; the pianist played three wrong notes but quickly regained his finesse, running his hands up and down the ivory keys. The commandant turned a critical eye toward the musician while Zohar poured the bubbly into eight glasses; he set on a walnut credenza.

Everyone picked up their champagne glasses, and the commandant toasted: "Here's to our most welcome guests."

"Cheers."

"Prost."

"Prost."

"You have a gorgeous home, Commandant," the major commented while admiring an ornately framed oil painting on a wall near the piano.

"Thank you, Major. That's an original Rembrandt, by the way. It's his *Holy Family with Angels*."

"I'm familiar with the painting," the major stated. "Tell me . . . how did you acquire such a rare and valuable piece of artwork?"

"It once belonged to a wealthy Jewish family who lived in Vienna."

"Serious art lovers, I gather?" the major questioned.

"That's right. The owner was the curator of the Wien art museum in Vienna. On the Karlsplatz."

"I know where it is, Commandant."

The major moved closer to the painting and saw that Rembrandt's signature had been scrawled on the bottom of the canvas.

"It's definitely authentic," he said. "It must have cost you a pretty penny. If you don't mind me asking—what was the price?"

The commandant grinned through his tightly clenched teeth. Before he answered, the commandant lit a smoke, sipped some more champagne, and then brushed a glittering piece of lint off his handsome dress uniform; he briefly noticed the unusual blue thread fall to the white granite floor.

"I didn't buy the painting, Major. We just removed it from the Jew's home."

"Oh?"

"The family had no use for it anymore," the commandant dryly stated. "Not where they were going."

"I see."

"The commandant has the loveliest furniture, Sergeant," Mrs. Himmel said, as the group migrated toward the lounge for appetizers and cocktails.

"*Danke schön*, Mrs. Himmel. We spent five tedious weeks decorating the house. The lounge is this way, ladies."

Mrs. Flügel whispered into Mrs. Segan's ear, "What do you suppose the sergeant meant by we? You don't think he and the commandant are married—do you?"

"It's always possible," Mrs. Segan replied, raising her wrist and flaunting her diamond-studded bracelet. "Come on, I'm thirsty. I need a good stiff drink already."

"Me too."

Decked in their shiny black shoes, tuxedo pants, shirts, and silk bow ties, Ben, Mr. Katz, and another prisoner from the camp readied themselves with trays in the lounge, preparing to serve the honored guests hot and cold delicacies: Swedish meatballs, pigs in a blanket, chicken liver in puff pastry, caviar on toast, smoked salmon canapes and deviled eggs.

"What would the lovely ladies like to drink?" the sergeant inquired, helping himself to a caviar on toast.

"A dry martini for me, please," the major's wife replied.

"I'll have a Bloody Mary. Bitte," Mrs. Flügel said.

"A scotch on the rocks," Mrs. Segan said.

"Make their drinks, Zugreb," the sergeant ordered.

"*Igen.*"

After Zohar made the women's cocktails, he served the lieutenant a gin and tonic and the captain a rum and coke. Major Himmel walked up to the bar and inquired, "Do you happen to have some of that American whiskey? You know, the one that's made in Tennessee."

Zohar reached for a bottle on the top shelf. He smiled and asked, "You mean Jack Daniels?"

"Yes, yes . . . with a couple of ice-cubes, *bitte*."

"Perhaps you would like a double, Major?"

"That would be excellent."

"Have you heard about the new mobile gassing units yet, Major?" Commandant Graben inquired.

Zohar served the major his drink.

"*Danke*. I haven't but I'm definitely interested in knowing more about them," the major replied. "Do they run on diesel or standard gasoline?"

"I believe diesel. But I could be wrong," the commandant answered. "Dachau recently acquired two of the units. They're finding them highly efficient. The gas chambers in the trucks are hermetically sealed and can fit maybe seventy victims inside. Once the poison gas is pumped in, the occupants are dead within ten or fifteen minutes."

"Saves on bullets," Sergeant Heimlich added with a smirk. "Would you like one of my American cigarettes, Major?"

"I don't smoke."

Ben came around with a tray of pigs in a blanket.

"I'll take one of those, Jew," the commandant said as he lifted one off the tray and dipped it in mustard.

Ben cordially offered one to the major.

"No, thank you. I'm a vegetarian."

"Our gas chamber has been running nonstop since we closed the one at Hartheim castle," the sergeant stated. "How long would it take for us to requisition a couple of those mobile units, Major?"

"I'm not sure. I'll look into it when we return to Berlin." The tall high-ranking officer stood and lifted his glass, "I would like to propose a toast."

Glowing elegantly in their evening wear, the officers' wives lifted their glasses along with everyone else.

Ben balanced his tray of appetizers and listened while Major Himmel spoke:

"To everyone's health. And a most enjoyable stay in Mauthausen."

"Prost, Major," the commandant said.

"Prost."

"Prost."

Sergeant Heimlich raised his cosmopolitan, and he also made a toast, "To the success of the final solution. May the Third Reich never rest until every Jew is wiped off the face of the planet."

"Prost, everyone," the commandant added.

"Prost."

"God forbid," Ben coughed under his breath.

The sergeant looked suspiciously at Ben; he inquired, "Did you say something, Weiss?"

"A pig in a blanket, sir?"

"Nein," the sergeant replied, as he rubbed his nose and mumbled pigdog in German, "*Schweinehund.*"

Major Himmel plopped on a bar stool, glanced down and admired the commandant's spiffy new boots.

"Where did you get those from?" the major asked.

The commandant threw back a scotch on the rocks, and signaled for Zohar to make him another.

"What are you referring to, Major?"

"Your boots. I love the style."

"Our shoemaker at the camp made them—how do they look on me?"

"Classy. He does excellent work," the major replied. "And … are they comfortable? Sometimes new boots tend to be a little stiff at first."

The commandant cleared his throat. "Pardon the cliché, Major. They fit like a glove."

"Could you arrange for your shoemaker to make me a pair?"

"Absolutely, Major. The shoemaker is standing right next to your wife. I'll call him over. You can speak to him yourself. Prisoner Katz, come over here, please."

Mr. Katz had a hearing disability in one ear, and he didn't readily respond. Plus, the saxophone jazz of Charlie Parker blared on a Victrola, making it even more difficult for him to hear.

"Katz!"

"Heimlich … do me a big favor?"

"Commandant?"

"Bring me that belligerent Jew—the shoemaker."

"*Ja.*"

Sergeant Heimlich approached Mr. Katz from behind and startled him by firmly rapping on his shoulder. He dropped a whole tray of caviar canapes onto the floor; some of the fish eggs spilled onto the bottom of Mrs. Flügel's red silk evening gown.

"*Schweinehund!*" the sergeant shouted. "Now look what you've done. Clean up this mess, Jew."

Mr. Katz quickly got on his hands and knees and picked up the food and nervously placed it onto the serving tray, while Ben dampened a napkin and offered to wipe Mrs. Flügel's evening gown.

The commandant walked over and asked, "What's going on here?"

"This dummkopf dropped a whole tray of expensive caviar," the sergeant replied. "Look . . . he stained the woman's dress."

"Don't be so hard on the man," Mrs. Flügel said. "It was only an accident."

The commandant whispered into the sergeant's ear, "Have the guards take him to the execution room immediately. And while you're at it—the piano player can go with him."

"Jawohl. Prisoner Weiss, finish cleaning this mess."

"I apologize for the inconvenience, Mrs. Flügel," the commandant said. "I'll have someone bring you more caviar right away."

"That won't be necessary—I've lost my appetite for your stinky fish eggs," she said before brusquely turning to the other women.

The sergeant pulled Mr. Katz off the floor. "Come with me."

The sergeant went into the living room and approached the wild-haired man who sat at the piano. He yanked him from the bench and took him and Mr. Katz outside to the wrap-around porch. The sergeant approached two guards who were smoking cigarettes.

"Bring these two Jews back to the camp and have them liquidated."

"*Jawohl,* Sergeant. With pleasure."

When they got to the camp, the guard escorted the piano player and Mr. Katz into a building, down a flight of stairs, and inside a dismal room where five other prisoners sat. One of the prisoners noticed the formally dressed men.

"You two look like you just came from a wedding."

"What is this place?" Mr. Katz asked him.

"The kapo said we were brought here to be photographed."

"Why?" the piano player inquired.

"I don't know. Better you not ask too many questions."

A kapo came into the room and tugged on the shirt of the man who sat next to Mr. Katz. He brought the man into a smaller room and seated him on a chair that sat flush against a wall. Above the chair, a round hole had been cut into the wall. A gun barrel was placed through the opening, and it pointed toward the back of the prisoner's head. The kapo ordered the prisoner, "Look at the camera and smile." The kapo left the cubicle. On the reverse side of the wall, someone pulled a trigger, killing the prisoner who was seated on the chair. The executioner went outside for a cigarette and fresh air while two prisoners removed the dead man from the cubicle, and another prisoner came in with a bucket of soapy water and quickly cleaned the bloody brains off the wall. After several minutes, the next victim was brought inside the execution room, and he was seated against the wall.

Back at the villa, the chef and his helpers made the final preparations for dinner while the commandant and the sergeant joked with the three high-ranking officers at the bar. Their wives sat at a table and socialized among themselves.

"What do you call a blind German, Sergeant?" the major asked.

"I give up—what?"

"A not see. Get it? Nazi!"

"Ha ha. Oh, that's pretty funny, Major," the commandant stated. "Another whiskey, Zohar."

"Did you hear the one about the—" the sergeant began, until Major Himmel interrupted him.

"What happened to that waiter, Sergeant?" the major asked.

"Which one?"

"The shoemaker. I wanted to speak to him about making me a pair of boots."

"He was taken to the execution room back at the camp."

"Are you out of your fucking minds?" the major shouted.

The three women looked uneasily toward the bar.

"He's probably dead by now," the sergeant nonchalantly stated, before downing a shot.

"What?" the major shouted again. "How will I get my boots made if you kill the shoemaker? Take me to this execution room immediately."

"But Major, we'll be having dinner soon," the commandant said.

"That's an order!"

"Take him there now, Sergeant," the commandant said. "And use my car; it'll be faster."

Meanwhile, back at the camp, a kapo escorted Mr. Katz inside the execution cubicle. He was told to sit on the chair against the wall, straighten his bowtie and smile for the fake camera.

The sergeant drove the black Mercedes through the camp's guard gate and quickly parked. He and the major hurried into a cold gray building. The odor of blood lingered in the air.

On the other side of the execution cubicle, a trigger was pulled but the chamber jammed. The executioner took out his revolver and was about to stick it through the hole when the major and the sergeant walked up behind him.

"Don't shoot!" the major exclaimed. "There's been a mistake. Release the prisoner."

The man turned around and saw the major and the sergeant in their military dress uniforms.

"I said release the prisoner—and bring him here," the major ordered once more.

"*Jawohl*. Kapo!"

A prisoner came running.

"*Ja?*"

"Take the man out and bring him here."

"Jawohl."

The kapo helped Mr. Katz off the chair and led him out by his arm. Mr. Katz questioned the major and the sergeant with a confused look. "What about the piano player? He's in there too," the shoemaker mentioned.

"Go get him, Sergeant," the major ordered.

The sergeant went into the waiting room and brought out the piano player. They took both prisoners outside and walked them to the car.

"Tuck in your shirts," the major ordered. "You're going back to work."

"We need to piss bad," Mr. Katz said before they got in the car.

"Do it right here. Quickly," the sergeant said.

On the drive back to the villa, Major Himmel turned around to the backseat and addressed Mr. Katz in Hungarian:

"I want you to make me a pair of dress boots like you made the commandant."

"I will have to measure your feet first."

"Of course. I'll meet you at your workbench tomorrow afternoon at five o'clock."

15

The next morning the high-ranking officers and their wives enjoyed a late continental breakfast in the dining room at Mauthausen. Major Himmel took a bite of his apricot strudel, before chasing it with a third double espresso. He turned to Lieutenant Flügel and informed him:

"I've decided to let you and Captain Segan handle the briefing scheduled with the commandant this afternoon. It's such a lovely day out, Greta and I will go for a relaxing ride through the countryside.

"*Jawohl*, Major."

"We should return sometime in the afternoon. Do you have any questions, Lieutenant?"

"*Nein*. Don't worry, Major. We will see to everything. You and your wife have yourselves a delightful day."

"*Danke schön.*"

Raphael drove the major's Mercedes along a country road which eventually led them through a charming village called Melk. Buildings with brick facades and wooden houses painted pink, white, brown, and yellow lined a cobblestoned main street. They slowly passed a grocery store and bakery; a post office; a French restaurant with a pair of white angel's wings on the window; a dry cleaner; and a barber shop. Some of the local inhabitants and shop owners stopped and gawked when the brightly painted automobile drove by them. Beyond the village, the major's car climbed a steep hill; at the top, a wooden sign pointed the direction to Saint Clemens Benedictine Monastery. Two large crosses were mounted high atop the terracotta roof of a massive building. Raphael parked and helped the major and his wife out.

"You can relax, Raphael. We should return in less than two hours."

"Very good, Major."

Major Himmel and his wife meandered past statues of saints posted at the front square of the sprawling abbey. A fountain of stone cherubs spit streams of water in the air. On the north side of the monastery, the River Danube splashed up along the abbey's broad foundation. The Austrian Alps loomed farther to the south; in the east, plumes of smoke hovered over Gusen, one of Mauthausen's sub-camps. The couple strolled arm-in-arm onto the grounds of Saint Clemens while the sun gradually approached its zenith.

Laboring in a vegetable garden nearby, four black-robed monks wielded a rake, shovel, spade, and water hose. They warily observed the unexpected visitors. The major and his wife sat on a bench underneath the shade of a leafy English oak. They heard a distant rumbling and watched as four B-17 bombers hovered over the horizon. The noisy aircraft boldly advanced like a rolling thunder; the monstrous air fleet passed overhead, leaving trails of thick cottonous exhaust. The major touched a strand of his wife's braided golden hair, and he breathed a deep sigh of relief. He contemplated the rich blueness of the late-morning sky.

"I'm really homesick, Greta."

"Me too, darling," she said. "Shall we go inside now?"

"*Ja.*"

The major and his wife left the wooden bench under the leafy oak, and they walked by a clock tower proximal to the front entrance. A young monk tolled the bell for high noon as the major knocked on a pink door. Moments later, a hooded monk appeared and greeted the unexpected guests.

"Heil Hellmenz. Can I help you, officer?"

"Good morning, brother. Or should I say good afternoon. My name is Major Wolfgang Himmel. And this is my wife, Greta."

"Pleased to meet you, Mr. and Mrs. Himmel. I'm Prior Mueller. What can I do for you, Major?"

The strong afternoon sunlight blurred the prior's vision some. He put up his hand to block the glare.

"Prior . . . I'm here on official business from Berlin, and we were just taking a leisurely ride through the countryside when we saw the monastery. We thought it would make an interesting place to visit since my wife and I are devout Catholics."

"That's a good thing, Major. But if the abbot isn't expecting you—I'm afraid we can't allow any visitors today."

"Not even a quick tour?" the major asked.

"We only give tours on Mondays, Tuesdays, and Saturdays," the prior said, growing more impatient.

"Are you sure you can't make an exception for us?" Mrs. Himmel pleaded. She charmingly smiled at the blond-bearded prior.

The prior frowned slightly, contemplating the major's authoritative red, black and white swastika armband.

"I don't make the rules at the monastery, Mrs. Himmel. I would need to check with the abbot first."

"We understand."

"Come inside, then," the prior said.

In the vestibule the vibrant noon light shone through a window below an arched ceiling. It illuminated the visitors' burnished faces. Mesmerized by their glowing countenances, Prior Mueller stepped back a moment and saw a halo of blue light around them.

"Is there something wrong, Prior?" the major asked.

"No. I just noticed that you both have very healthy-looking skin. Wait here while I look for the abbot."

Abbot Zebedee was not inside his office, so the prior closed the door and continued through the hallway until he came to a spiral staircase that circled high above. Painted on the ceiling atop the stairwell, frescoes exploded with vivid colors and seraphic themes. The prior held onto a wrought-iron handrail and cautiously ascended the tedious metal stairs. It was a long way up and a long way down. After climbing the numerous steps, the prior reached the top floor, where a voluminous library was housed. He entered a room filled with tall bookshelves, murals, and windows that offered panoramic views of the village, the River Danube, and the Austrian Alps. The prior passed the librarian's desk and walked through the inner sanctum of the book room. He approached a scholarly man of great stature, who was sitting at a table and studying an ancient Latin manuscript.

"I had an inkling you might be up here," the prior greeted the man of great stature. "I'm sorry if I disturbed you."

"What is it now, Mueller?" Abbot Zebedee asked.

The broad Italian abbot uncovered his hood, removed his reading glasses, and pensively rolled his eyes up at his blond-bearded assistant.

"A Nazi officer and his wife are waiting for you downstairs in the vestibule."

"What on earth for?"

"He asked to meet with you. Perhaps get a look around the abbey."

"Why didn't you tell him I was busy?"

"I tried . . . but they were persistent. Said they were devout Catholics," the prior said.

"Tell him to get lost. You know we don't give tours on Wednesdays. And since when have Nazis ever been devout Catholics? Seems a bit ironic to me."

Abbot Zebedee turned a page in the manuscript, put on his reading glasses again, and focused on the Latin text.

"He came from Berlin, Abbot. He said he was a high-ranking officer."

"Big deal. What am I supposed to do with these God-damn

Nazis already? Royal pains in my ass. Forgive me, Lord. Go downstairs and accompany them to my office. Heat up some water in the tea kettle. And tell the *Capitan* and his wife I'll be there shortly."

The prior corrected the abbot before leaving, "I believe he said he was a major."

"What's the difference?" the abbot asked. "They're all rotten scumbags to me," he said under his breath. "Murderous lot. Forgive me, Lord."

The abbot made the sign of the cross, closed the manuscript and slowly raised his large body off the chair. He plodded toward the librarian's desk, where Brother Martin was reading about Abraham and his wife, Sara. He raised his eyes to the abbot.

"It's utterly amazing how Abraham's wife was able to conceive a child at ninety years old," the librarian stated. "It's downright miraculous."

"Yes, it is, Brother Martin. Miraculous. Have a blessed afternoon."

"You as well, Abbot. Be careful going down the stairs."

"Always."

The abbot lifted his robe with one hand and securely held the handrail with the other. He descended the spiral staircase, adoring the murals along the way. At the bottom step he paused to catch his breath and wipe his brow. The hem of his robe swished back and forth as he moved through the hallway. He opened the door to his office and saw the Nazi officer and his wife seated there.

"Ah, greetings. And welcome to Saint Clemens Monastery. I'm Abbot Zebedee."

The major stood and politely shook the abbot's broad hand.

"It's a pleasure to make your acquaintance, Abbot. My name is Major Himmel. And this is my wife, Greta."

She smiled, removed her sun hat, stood, and offered the abbot her soft hand. The abbot held it gently and felt a warmth of energy a few moments. He saw that the woman's eyes gave off a peculiar blue scintillation.

The tea kettle whistled.

"Sit," the abbot said, motioning to the chairs. "Will you and your wife be joining me for a cup of tea?"

"That would be most gracious of you," the major replied.

"Prior, would you prepare three teas, please."

"Yes, of course."

"And what can I do for you, Major? I understand that you and your wife are interested in a tour of the monastery?"

"That won't be necessary, Abbot. Perhaps at a more convenient time. The main reason I'm here concerns the war effort."

"And how is that going?" the clergyman asked.

"War is a filthy business, Abbot. I'd much rather see peace in Europe. I can never understand why humans kill each other. When you come right down to it, we're all just brothers and sisters on God's good earth."

"I definitely agree with you there," the abbot said, maneuvering his large body around to sit on a chair at his desk.

The prior asked, "Would our guests like sugar or honey in their tea? We make the honey at the monastery. Well . . . the bees do most of the actual work."

"A teaspoon of honey in both cups, please," the major replied.

The prior opened a jar of clover honey, added the sweetener, and then handed the major and his wife the teacups.

"*Danke schön.*"

"*Bitte schön.*"

"I've come here with a specific purpose in mind," Major Himmel announced.

"And what might that be?" the abbot asked.

"You must be familiar with Mauthausen."

"I grew up in the village," the abbot said. "I know the place like the back of my hand. My parents moved there from Rome when I was five."

"I meant the concentration camp," the major stated.

"Unfortunately, I am familiar with the camp. When the wind

blows wrong, the smoke from the crematorium seeps into the monastery. It's a most unpleasant experience."

"I'm sure of that," the major stated.

The abbot asked the prior to give him and his guests some privacy. "Prior, could you go to town and buy some milk, please? Here's the car keys."

"Yes, of course, Abbot. It was a pleasure meeting you and your wife, Major."

"Likewise."

Prior Mueller left the office and slowly closed the door. He stood in the hallway a few moments, hoping to catch some of the conversation inside. He put his ear against the door. Sister Hildegard saw him as she strolled through the hallway. The nun gave the eavesdropping prior a disdainful glance.

"Shame on you, Prior—you know better than that."

He embarrassingly put his head down and quickly walked away.

Inside the office, the abbot grew more fidgety with his guests. Major Himmel patiently set his cup down, noticing a painting of the Vatican. He smiled at his wife.

"I'm going to bring you three Hungarian prisoners from the Mauthausen camp," the major announced.

"What on earth for?"

"The commandant and I have decided they should work at the monastery."

"That's sort of odd," the abbot stated. "What kind of work do the prisoners do?"

"One's a shoemaker, an electrician, and a glazier. They're decent and hardworking men. And I'm sure there's plenty of work for them to do around here."

"There is . . . but I don't know if it's such a good idea for Jews to come here and work," the abbot said.

"Why not? They can live at the monastery as well. It'd be more convenient for them."

The abbot scratched his large head and stirred his tea. He took a sip and looked at the major.

"I'd have to think it over first."

"Unfortunately, you don't have that option, Abbot. I've already made arrangements with the commandant at Mauthausen."

The abbot was befuddled.

"This is all so sudden."

"Don't worry—it's all for a good cause."

"The war effort?" the abbot asked.

"So to speak."

"How long will they be at the monastery?" the abbot inquired.

"That all depends on how long the war lasts."

"When will the prisoners be coming?"

"Tomorrow morning before sunrise," the major replied. "You'll receive them yourself. And provide them with three private rooms, meals, and clothing like the other monks wear. You'll treat them as if they were monks. And nobody at the monastery can know they came from Mauthausen. All except for Sister Hildegard. She can be trusted to tell. But definitely not Prior Mueller. If anyone asks you about the three new monks, tell them they were formerly at the Archabbey in Pannonhalma, in Hungary. Like I said before, the three men are Hungarian. Do you understand me, Abbot?"

"I do."

"Good. I'll need from you three monk's robes and three pairs of shoes," the major said. "Write all these sizes down."

The abbot picked up a pencil and found some note paper.

"One man is tall. He should fit into a large robe. The other two robes would be a medium and a small. Their shoe sizes are seven, eight, and ten. Put the large size shoes with the large robe, the eight with the medium, and the seven with the small robe. They'll need new undergarments and socks as well. All the clothing and shoes should be placed in separate garment bags if you have them. I'll need it all now. After the clothes have been organized, my driver will help bring it out to the car."

The abbot picked up his phone. "I'll call the laundry and have someone prepare the clothes now."

"Excellent," the major said while he reached into his pants

pocket and took out a brown envelope; he set it in front of the abbot.

After the abbot spent a few minutes on the phone, he hung up the receiver and asked the major about the envelope.

"What's that for?"

"Open it."

The abbot tore open the envelope and found a thick wad of money in large denominations. "What's this?"

"Ten thousand deutsche marks," the major stated. "A little donation for the monastery."

"Oh, that's most generous of you, Major! Thank you very much. I have gifts for you also," the abbot said, as he reached for a bottle on the shelf behind him. He smiled and set the bottle in front of the major. "It's from my private stock."

"Ah! Wunderbar. Benedictine and brandy," the major said. "Thank you, Abbot."

"You're welcome. And take this, Mrs. Himmel," he said, giving her a small bible inscribed with gold words. Saint Clemens Monastery.

"Oh . . . danke schön."

"Bitte schön."

"If it's possible, Abbot . . . my wife and I would like to pray in your chapel before we leave. We're both devout Catholics."

"Yes, of course, the prior informed me. Come with me; I'll show you where it is."

The major grabbed the Benedictine and Brandy while his wife placed the small bible in her pocketbook.

At five o'clock that afternoon in the camp's maintenance building, Ben cut a pane of glass and gently set it into a window frame; he smoothed a ribbon of putty along the edges and placed the repaired window aside. He lifted another window frame onto the worktable and proceeded to remove the hardened putty with a hammer and chisel. A welder looked up from his workbench, scattering orange sparks in the air. Major Himmel entered the building, and most everyone stood at attention. Two carpenters paused from hammering three-penny nails into a truss, and the shrill sound of a circular saw came to a stop. Zohar, the electrician, interrupted his tinkering of the commandant's short-wave radio. He had tuned in a station from Berlin but silenced the Führer's screaming voice through the static on the speaker. Mr. Katz stopped hammering a sole onto a boot, when the major walked over to the cobbler's workbench.

"Good afternoon, Prisoner Katz. How are you doing today?"

"Good afternoon, Major. I'm doing fine—thanks to you. Have a seat and I'll take those measurements now."

The major smiled, took off his cap, and sat on a chair. Mr. Katz raised one of the major's legs onto a short stool and removed his old boot. He took the other one off and proceeded to measure the length and width of the officer's feet. He wrote the dimensions on a piece of scrap paper.

"Do you want them with a zipper on the side?" the shoemaker asked.

"That'll be fine."

"Black or brown leather?"

"I prefer brown," the major said.

Mr. Katz added that info onto the scrap paper, and he put the officer's old boots back on.

"You're all set then," the shoemaker said. "They should be ready for you next week. Do you want them mailed to Berlin?"

"I'm not in a rush, brother Katz. I'll get them when I see you at the monastery."

The shoemaker looked up, puzzled. "I don't understand, Major—what do you mean by monastery?"

"I'll explain. Call the electrician and the glazier over here."

"Ben! Zohar!" Mr. Katz shouted above the noise inside the building. He waved to them. The two men stopped working, and they met at the cobbler's workbench.

"First off, I want to compliment everyone on the tremendous job you did on the party last night," the major said. "Each of you grab a milk crate and sit."

Ben and Zohar found milk crates and placed them by the shoemaker's workbench.

The major spoke in a fluent Hungarian.

"The commandant and I have decided to give the three of you new work assignments. You're going to work at a monastery a few kilometers from here. It's called Saint Clemens. Very nice place. We've arranged for you to live there as well. Don't tell anyone in the camp you're leaving. Guards or otherwise. That's very important."

"What kind of work will it be, Major?" Zohar asked.

"The same work you're doing here."

"What about tools?" Ben asked. "We have none of our own."

"You'll take the tools from here, but only what fits into a milk crate. Everything else you'll need, the monastery will provide. While you're at the abbey you'll say absolutely nothing about the concentration camp. Nothing at all. And if anyone asks, you'll tell them you've never heard of Mauthausen. You will pretend to be Benedictine monks while you're there. And have recently come from the Archabbey of Pannonhalma in Hungary. That's Archabbey of Pannonhalma. Does everyone understand my Hungarian?" the major asked through the workers' din.

The three men acknowledged that they did.

"Are there any more questions?"

"When do we start work at the monastery?"

"The day after you arrive there, Brother Benjamin. "Tomorrow at four in the morning, before anyone else gets here, the three of you will come and pack your tools. I'll meet you here and my driver will take you to Saint Clemens. Remember, not a word of this to anyone. Have a good evening, brothers. Lock your lockers. I believe it's time for roll call," the major said as a loud bell rang inside the maintenance building.

16

June 6, 1944

D-Day

In the muted darkness of Barracks 20, Ben tiredly climbed down from the top bunk while the three-hundred or more other prisoners slept, all except for a few inmates who were secretively masturbating underneath their lice-ridden blankets. Ben securely placed his watch into his pants pocket before putting on his grubby canvas shoes and cotton cap. He gently shook Mr. Katz's arm and whispered, "Wake up, it's time to go, brother."

"Okay . . ."

They went to the communal wash area, where Zohar was already shaving in a small handheld mirror. He raised his eyes to the men but remained silent. A naked prisoner nearby was puking into a toilet; he glanced at the men before going back to what he was doing.

Not wanting to arouse much attention, they exited the barracks five minutes apart. Zohar left first, Ben second, and Mr. Katz last. All of them showed their camp passes to the barely responsive kapo who was on duty by the barracks door. A Nazi guard was passed out in his chair, an empty whiskey bottle on the floor next to him. The camp lights weren't on outside, including the ones in the guard towers. One by one, the three men felt their way into the dark maintenance building, only turning on the single light bulb above their workstations. They packed tools into their wooden milk crates, and by four o'clock, Major Himmel arrived. He shined a bright flashlight through the doorway.

"Hurry, men. Take your boxes and follow me," the major ordered.

They went outside and loaded their milk crates into the trunk of the idling Mercedes. It was very dark out, yet Ben and the other two men noticed a distinct blue haze around the automobile.

"Get in the car," the major said.

The major's driver wiped away a grayish white chimney ash from the side-view mirrors; he closed the trunk and the doors and then sat behind the wheel. The *Kübelwagen* escorted the major's vehicle through the open guard gate, and the half-conscious sentry there lethargically waved. The two vehicles sped through the sleepy village of Mauthausen. After twenty minutes they quietly pulled onto a dirt road and switched off their headlights. They rolled a quarter kilometer past a farmhouse and stopped shortly thereafter. The major turned on the overhead light while Raphael got out and opened the trunk.

"The clothes you'll be wearing at the monastery are in three garment bags in the trunk," the major said. "Your names are on the bags. Go outside and change. Put your prison uniforms and shoes into the empty garment bags. After, pile the bags onto the side of the road. Do it fast—now."

While Ben, Zohar, and Mr. Katz put on their new clothing, a woman illuminated a porch light from the farmhouse down the road. She yelled, and a dog barked. A man came out and fired a hunting rifle.

"Hurry, men," the major said, as he got out of the car. He waited until they filled the garment bags and stacked them on the side of the road. The major felt a bullet whiz past his ear. "Get in the car—hurry."

The new monks lifted the bottoms of their black robes and

climbed inside the bulletproof limo. The major opened a small jar that contained gasoline; he poured the fuel over the garment bags and struck a match to the pile. It blazed a bright orange. The major got back in the car.

"Drive, Raphael."

The vehicles put on their lights and swiftly turned around and drove down the dirt road. A bullet bounced off the Mercedes's rear window as they pulled onto the highway again.

Ben smelled the spicey clean material on the black robe he was wearing. The cloth was much more comfortable than the scratchy prison uniforms they left burning.

Farther along the route, an English broadcaster excitedly announced from the radio inside the major's limo, "Good morning. This is John Snagge from the BBC in London. I've just been informed that the American, British, and Canadian airborne troops have landed on the beaches of Normandy, France, early this morning. D-day has begun! I repeat. D-day has begun!"

"The allies are in France, Ben," Zohar whispered.

"Oh?"

"*Igen.*"

The major smiled, closed his eyes, and then took a brief nap.

The Mercedes and the military vehicle traveled a few more kilometers before entering the village of Melk. They went through the town, accelerated to the top of a steep hill, and parked in front of Saint Clemens Monastery. A speck of orange-yellow light appeared on the horizon. The major's chauffeur stepped out and opened the trunk. He unloaded the three milk crates, closed the trunk, and opened the back doors.

The major turned around, "Be sure to do good work, brothers. Farewell. And may God be with you always."

He made the sign of the cross, and the three men climbed from the car without saying a word. Raphael smiled at them, closed the doors, and got behind the wheel again. Abbot Zebedee stood by the front entrance and waved to Major Himmel. He waved back.

The major and his driver put on dark sunglasses, and the two vehicles headed toward the rising sun.

Ben, Mr. Katz, and Zohar picked up their boxes and approached the man of great stature.

"Ah . . . the monks from Pannonhalma Archabbey are here. Welcome to Saint Clemens Monastery. Come in, brothers. Leave your things in the hall for now," he said. The abbot shut the thick wooden door and locked it. "My name is Abbot Zebedee. I'm in charge of the monastery. Introduce yourselves, brothers."

"I'm Brother Benjamin."

He and the abbot shook hands.

"You have a powerful grip, my friend. And what is your occupation?"

"I'm a glazier."

"Good. We have many broken windows at the monastery," the abbot stated. He turned to the tallest man. "And what is your name and occupation, my friend?"

"Brother Zohar. I'm an electrician."

"Excellent. We have much electrical work that needs updating here."

Zohar smiled, and the two men shook hands.

And who are you, brother?" the abbot inquired.

"My name is Brother Jacob, Your Majesty."

"The shoemaker, I assume?"

"Yes, Your Majesty."

"I'm not a king, Brother Jacob. Just a humble abbot. No reason for the majesty."

"Yes, sir."

"I'm pleased to meet you all," the abbot said. "We'll go to my office now and drink coffee. Come . . . it's right this way."

While they drank their coffees, the abbot opened a top desk drawer, and he took out three wood crosses on beaded necklaces. He handed each man one.

"Your train ride from Hungary must have been exhausting," the broad Italian abbot said. "Put the necklaces on. And only take them off when you have a bath or go to sleep. You're Jews, so wearing a cross will undoubtedly feel strange at first."

"I'm a Protestant," Brother Zohar stated.

"Good. I'll teach everyone the sign of the cross," the abbot said.

He proceeded to show them the movements of the ritual a few times. The men mimicked him. The abbot smiled and sipped his coffee.

"I think you've got the hang of it. I'm certain you'll all adapt well to the customs at Saint Clemens. Just be careful of what you say when you're around the other brothers and sisters. And don't mention anything about the concentration camp. Especially to Prior Mueller. You'll probably meet him soon. He's my assistant at the abbey. Major Himmel may have informed you already, but if anyone asks, you've come from the Archabbey in Pannonhalma. That's, the Archabbey in Pannonhalma. Memorize it well, brothers. Be sure to follow how the other monks behave around the monastery. You should be fine."

When Prior Mueller finished his early morning prayers, he closed his breviary, left the chapel, and then proceeded down the hallway toward the front vestibule. He wondered why the three milk crates were on the floor, noticing the tools inside the boxes. He walked to the abbot's office and knocked.

"Come in."

"Why are those milk crates in the foyer, Abbot?" the prior asked. "Oh! Good morning. I'm sorry, Abbot . . . didn't know you would have company this early."

The three new monks were rehearsing the sign of the cross. The prior looked at them, smiled, and then returned the ritual.

"Good morning, Prior," the abbot greeted. "These are the three new brothers from the Archabbey in Pannonhalma, I told you about yesterday. May I introduce you to Brother Benjamin, Brother Jacob, and this is Brother Zohar."

The abbot nodded to each of them in turn.

"Welcome, brothers. I'm Prior Mueller."

They all shook hands, and the prior observed the men's

exhausted faces; he felt the scrapes and calluses on their palms when their hands touched.

"Prior, after the brothers have had their coffee, they'll take their tools, and you'll show them where their workbenches are in the basement."

"Yes, Abbot. Where will they be staying?"

"I prepared the three end rooms on the top floor. Give them clean towels and soap and show them where they can bathe. Afterward, you'll bring them down to breakfast. They've had an arduous journey from Hungary. I'm sure they must be famished. Once they've eaten, tell Brother Joseph to give them a full tour of the monastery," Abbot Zebedee said. "I'll be up in the library if I'm needed. Have a blessed day everyone."

17

Commandant Graben turned over in his bed and dreamt he was trapped inside a thick glass paperweight, similar to the one he had on his desk at the camp, only a much larger version of it. He banged on the glass and called for help while snowflakes fell on top of his head. On the outside of the glass three Santa Clauses laughed and waved to the commandant. He watched a big yellow carp swim by. And the nightmare ended.

Sergeant Heimlich shouted into the bedroom phone, then slammed down the receiver.

"What's wrong, Sergeant?"

"Corporal Wagner just informed me that a few hundred prisoners escaped from the camp last night."

"What!"

"Officers from the Russian compound and several Hungarian prisoners from Barracks 20," the sergeant said.

"How did that happen?"

The commandant climbed out of bed and put on his bathrobe and slippers. He reached for a cigarette.

"Give me a light."

"He said the guards on duty this morning found gaping holes cut into the electric fences," the sergeant replied, "Someone rigged the breaker box for the entire camp, and the power and lights went off last night. The guards in the watchtowers were found asleep early this morning. They may have been drugged."

"Drugged?"

"Some kind of strong sedative," the sergeant replied.

"Get me a coffee. I'm taking a shower."

The sergeant and the commandant stood on the front porch of the villa, and they noticed that the military vehicle and the major's bright blue Mercedes were gone from the driveway.

"Our guests must be having an early breakfast at the camp," the commandant said. "Let's see what's going on with this escape."

They got into the commandant's Mercedes, and the sergeant rode the brake down the steep driveway.

"So, how was the meeting yesterday?" Heimlich inquired.

"Fine. Just odd that Major Himmel didn't attend. I gave the other two officers and their wives a tour of the camp. Before they leave, I'll be having lunch with the major and his wife."

"Where at?"

"The Ailes d'ange," Commandant Graben replied. "The major said he and his wife love French food, so I thought I'd take them there. He wants to brief me on some plans about a super rocket the Führer's scientists have been developing at the sub-camp near Melk."

"The Gusen camp?"

"*Ja.* Top secret."

The sergeant approached the front guard gate and stopped. Corporal Wagner focused through his thick eyeglasses to see who they were.

"Heil Hellmenz, Commandant, Sergeant."

"Any news about the escaped prisoners?" the commandant inquired.

"Several were found dead outside the camp's perimeter. The mayor of Mauthausen called me five minutes ago. Said a large group of prisoners were wandering around the village. Looking for food and water."

"Have you seen Major Himmel and his group?" the sergeant asked.

"*Nein.*"

"Let's go, Sergeant."

They drove into the camp and parked next to a rusted blue motorcycle with a sidecar attached. The two men got out and stared at the vehicle.

"Who does that belong to?" the commandant asked.

"I don't know . . . I've never seen it here before."

"Strange," the commandant stated. "I want you to form a work crew, Heimlich. Have them collect the prisoners who died by the camp's perimeter. Burn the bodies. Get a manhunt organized immediately. Contact Mayor Fickmich in Mauthausen and tell him to recruit a large group of men—the Nazi youth brigade can join them as well. We'll need tracking dogs too. After roll call, I want every god-damn prisoner stripped naked and moved to the garage yard. Have a firing squad shoot the remaining prisoners from Barracks 20 and the Russian compound."

"*Ja.*"

Like a crazed Nazi, Sergeant Heimlich swung his arms up and down and high-stepped into the maintenance building. He stomped over to the shoemaker's workbench and noticed his tool locker had been left open. All the shoemaking tools and shoe leather was gone. A lone shoehorn remained behind. The angry sergeant inspected the electrician's work area next. It was a mess. Wires were everywhere, locker open, and everything missing except for a powerful hand tool used to cut through metal fences like butter. Zohar's yellow work pass was taped to his locker; someone had drawn a caricature of the Fuhrer's rabid-looking face on it. At Ben's well-organized worktable, the sergeant picked up the empty box the glass cutters had come in. He looked inside the glazier's locker and found that it was emptied of its contents. The sergeant kicked over a mirror and asked a Spanish welder if he had seen anything unusual the last couple of days.

"*Nein*, Sergeant."

The welder smiled, pursed his lips, and then returned to his work.

The commandant stormed into the administration building and knocked on his secretary's door.

"Enter."

"Have you seen the dignitaries from Berlin?"

"*Nein,* Commandant. There was an escape last night," Mrs. Holstein said while she nonchalantly painted her fingernails.

"I was informed of it already."

"Someone left you a package by your door," she announced.

"Who's it from?"

"I don't know," she impudently replied. "It was here when I arrived this morning."

"Major Himmel and his wife will be coming in today. I'll need you to make a good impression. And . . . eh . . . I hope you remembered to put your underpants on this morning, Mrs. Holstein."

"Yes, Commandant, I have them on. Would you like to see? They're black and made out of silk."

"That won't be necessary. What's that scent?" he asked, sniffing the sweetly perfumed air.

"Patchouli. Do you like it?"

"It's nice. A bit on the heavy side though."

The commandant left his secretary's office and picked up the package outside his door. He brought it inside, set it on his desk, and pulled out a bottle of Benedictine and Brandy. He read the note attached to the bottle.

Dear Commandant Graben,

Thank you for your most generous hospitality. I'm sorry to inform you but due to unforeseen circumstances, I must cancel our luncheon for today. The other officers and I were summoned back to Berlin immediately.

All the best,

Major Wolfgang Himmel
Office of the High Command in Berlin

Sergeant Heimlich rushed into the commandant's office.

"I have some more bad news, Commandant."

"What is it now?"

"The glazier, the shoemaker, and the electrician must have escaped last night. They weren't at roll call this morning."

"Have you checked the maintenance building?"

"They weren't there either. And their tools are missing."

"*Schweinhunds!*" the commandant shouted, crumpling the major's note in his hand. "Is that group for the manhunt ready yet?"

"Almost. I spoke with Mayor Fickmich ten minutes ago. I'll be going with them."

"*Gut.* Be sure to search every house and farm in the area, Sergeant. I want those prisoners hunted down and butchered like pigs. Understand?"

"*Ja.* Who gave you the gift?" the sergeant asked, noticing the liquor bottle on the desk.

"The major! Now get that fucking manhunt organized, or you'll be working in the quarry today."

After the sergeant left the commandant's office, Graben picked up and shook his heavy glass paperweight. He observed the miniature winter landscape and suddenly recalled the bizarre dream he had last night. He flung the heavy object across the room, and it busted the glass on his aquarium. The water gushed out onto the floor and took the tropical fish with it.

In the pandemonium filled town hall of Mauthausen, soldiers, thirty boys from the Nazi youth movement, a few dozen concerned citizens, and several farmers with their older sons gathered with military weapons, hunting rifles, pistols, machetes, axes, pitchforks, and wooden clubs. Outside, fifty cigarette-smoking Gestapo held vigil, while they restrained their leashed and salivating Bloodhounds, Doberman Pinschers and German Shepherds. Sergeant Heimlich signaled to the large group inside the town hall, and the raucous mob burst through the doorway. They loaded onto trucks, motorcycles and cars while the corpulent mayor and sheriff of Mauthausen remained at the town hall, where they stuffed themselves with a breakfast of sweet pastries and goose liver. Afterward, they washed it down with a frothy German lager.

A military vehicle drove around the village of Mauthausen; a loudspeaker blared from its roof:

"The escaped prisoners are armed and dangerous criminals. Do not to go near, feed, give shelter, or help the criminals in any manner whatsoever," a soldier announced through the loudspeaker. "Anyone found aiding the escaped prisoners will suffer dire consequences."

The military vehicle drove along another street, broadcasting the same message.

Sergeant Heimlich and an SS officer commandeered the manhunt from the sergeant's Kübelwagen. The riotous mob swiftly found a couple dozen escapees slumped on stoops, benches, gutters, and beside the tracks at the Mauthausen train station. They slaughtered the hatchet-faced pajama-dressed men where they rested. The hundred or more members on the manhunt broke off into splinter groups, and the bloodletting search proceeded to the next locale.

At a dairy farm right outside the town, a soldier smashed his gloved fist on a farmhouse door while a few Nazi youths investigated the property and barn.

"Open the door!" a soldier yelled.

The farmer's wife appeared with a frightened look on her face. She was dressed in coveralls and a kitchen apron.

"Can I help you?" she asked the young soldier.

"We're looking for the prisoners who escaped from Mauthausen last night. Are any of the killers here?"

"Killers? Of course not," she replied. "We have no killers here."

The soldier ogled the farmer's wife. "You're a beautiful woman."

"I'm married," she said, showing the soldier her ring.

"Give me coffee," the unwelcome Gestapo ordered as he barged into the home. She showed him where the kitchen was, and he sat at the table. She made a pot of fresh coffee, boiled some eggs, and then sliced some fresh-baked brown bread. The soldier's cigarette smoke filled the room while he impatiently drummed his fingers on the table. He asked, "And where is your husband, pretty woman?"

"Working in the barn. He should be done soon."

The farmer finished milking his cows and tiredly walked into the house. He coughed from the tobacco smoke. Shocked to see a Nazi soldier sitting at his kitchen table and flirting with his wife, the farmer asked his wife: "What are these people doing here, Elsa?"

The soldier gobbled another hard-boiled egg. He washed it down with coffee.

"There was an escape from the camp last night. The murderers are everywhere. Jews. They are armed and dangerous. We must search your house."

"This is a farm," the husband stated. "We have no murderers here."

"We shall see," the Nazi said as got up from the table. He left the kitchen and headed for a staircase.

The farmer's wife put her hand over her mouth in fear. The soldier stomped upstairs to a bedroom, where he found two young children asleep. He looked under their bed, checked the closets, and then inspected the master bedroom. The soldier came downstairs and sat at the kitchen table again.

Three teenage Nazi youths came inside and searched the basement. It didn't take long for them to discover two men cowering underneath some dirt in a root cellar. The youths pulled the men out and led them upstairs.

"What do we have here?" the soldier questioned. "I thought you said there wasn't anyone in the house. You lied!"

The farmer's wife noticed the yellow stars that were sewn onto the two men's shirts. Her heart sank.

"This is a serious crime, protecting Jews," the soldier said.

"We didn't know they were here—they must have gotten into the house last night," the farmer's wife stated. "While we were sleeping. We didn't hear anyone come in."

"And we never lock our doors," the Austrian farmer added.

"No? I don't believe you!" the soldier exclaimed. "You and your family are under arrest for harboring escaped prisoners."

"Our family? Honestly. Please. We didn't know they were down there," the farmer pleaded.

"Take the two prisoners outside and shoot them," the Gestapo ordered the three Nazi youth. "Go with them," he told the farmer.

"*Jawohl, Capitan,*" the older of the three boys said. "*Rouse, Juden.*"

When they left, the young soldier grabbed the farmer's wife by the hand; he took her upstairs and raped her in the master bedroom. Afterward, the entire family was taken away to the concentration camp nearby. They were never heard from again.

The manhunt moved on to the next farmhouse and village. Bloodthirsty dogs tracked the scent of the escaped prisoners, leading the mobs through the forest. They hunted the men past sundown, through the night, and into the following day. Most of the escaped prisoners had been rounded up and murdered. Less than a dozen escaped capture. More than two hundred were left dead on the roadsides, farms, and streets of the quaint Austrian villages and throughout the surrounding woods. For two days, camp prisoners, farmers, and the people of the towns loaded the emaciated corpses onto trucks and wagons. The dead were transported to empty fields, where earth-digging vehicles hollowed out long burial trenches. Dump trucks delivered the rest of the corpses back to Mauthausen's sub-camps, where they were burned to ash in the ovens.

Back at his private villa, Commandant Graben poured some

Benedictine and Brandy into three glasses. He handed one to an exhausted Sergeant Heimlich, and one to the SS officer who had been in charge of the manhunt. They raised their glasses.

"To a job well done," the commandant toasted.

"*Danke schön. Prost.*"

"*Prost.*"

The three men drank up and laughed as the bar filled with a foggy thick cigar smoke.

"You found them all, Franz?" the commandant asked the SS officer.

"*Nein,*" he replied. "The Russian officers are history. All except for six or seven we couldn't locate. Three Hungarian prisoners from Barracks 20 are still unaccounted for."

"What are their names?" the commandant curiously inquired.

"Zugreb, Katz, and Weiss," the SS officer replied.

"Keep looking for them, Franz. When you find these three prisoners, bring them back to me alive. I will castrate them myself."

"*Jawohl.*"

The commandant angrily jabbed the point of a long knife into the bar. He picked up the liquor bottle and refilled the three glasses.

18

Almost to the end of his first day at the monastery, Ben meditated by a quickening twilight in the chapel, when a white pigeon startled him by erratically flying in circles directly above his head. He flailed his arms and attempted to shoo away the creature. An elderly monk stood by and clapped his hands twice; the fine-feathered friend flew up toward a broken stained-glass window. Where it softly cooed.

"They're harmless. Although annoying," the older monk said, offering to shake Ben's hand. "I'm Brother Zebulon. You must be the new monk in town."

"I am. I'm Brother Benjamin."

"Where do you come from, brother?"

"Hungary. The Archabbey of Pannonhalma."

"It's nice meeting you, brother. Have a peaceful evening."

"You, as well."

Ben sat again, looked above, and continued with his thoughts. He wondered about his mother and father's whereabouts, as well as that of his siblings. He missed them all. *Papa wouldn't have endured a single day's work at Mauthausen. And no women there were Mama's age. Maybe they were taken to the camp the sergeant had spoken about.* He didn't want to think the worst. Not knowing really troubled him. His heart filled with a melancholy.

A sister entered the shadowy chapel, and she lit some votive candles on a credenza by the large oak doors. Brother Benjamin looked at the lights, and the sister noticed his worried disposition. More monks and nuns entered the chapel. Brother Jacob tapped on Ben's shoulder, and he sat on his right side, while Brother Zohar sat on his left. Vespers had begun.

After evening prayers, the three new monks departed the chapel and climbed the staircase to the third floor, where they bid each other a good night.

Inside his tiny monk's quarters, Ben turned on a lamp on the small desk and noticed a pen and note with someone's handwriting.

> Dear Brother Benjamin,
>
> Welcome to Saint Clemens Monastery.
> Wishing your stay here, only be filled with blessings and joy.
>
> Sincerely,
> Abbot Zebedee, and all the brothers and sisters at Saint Clemens

After reading the kind message, Ben's heart uplifted somewhat. He removed his watch from his robe pocket and saw that it was eight o'clock. He undressed and removed the cross from around his neck; he placed it and the watch on the desk before darkening the lamp. Ben happily collapsed onto the small but comfortable bed. The first one he would be sleeping in since leaving home in Beregszász.

The sounds of distant bombing and air-raid sirens disturbed Ben's deep sleep. He opened his eyes, and his second day in the monastery had begun. He got out of bed and searched for the lamp on the desk. He turned on the light, dressed, put on the necklace, and opened his gold pocket watch; it was nothing short of a miracle he still owned it. The hour was five o'clock. He placed the watch in his robe pocket, put on his shoes, and then hurried to the bathroom down the hall.

When Ben returned to his room, Zohar was standing by his door, tall and dignified, dressed in his long black monk's robe. Ben thought the religious apparel suited the man well.

"Good morning, Brother Zohar."

"Morning, brother . . . I have some good news for you."

"Come in for a minute. We can talk inside."

While Ben made his bed, Zohar inspected his clean-shaven face in the mirror. A framed portrait of Christ hung beside it.

"How do you like your room, Ben? Mine feels kind of small."

"That's because you're so tall—what about the good news, Zohar?"

"The American and British forces have advanced last night. They succeeded in breaching Germany's coastal defense of France. Not without casualties, unfortunately. A few thousand allied soldiers died."

"Oh." Ben tied his shoelaces. "Who told you that?"

"I heard it on the BBC last night. The station came in loud and clear."

"From the radio in the dining room?"

"The commandant's short-wave radio," Zohar replied. "I packed it in the milk crate by mistake. I finally fixed it last night."

"Don't let anyone know you have it, or we'll all be in trouble."

"I keep the volume down low. And I have a good hiding place for it."

"Be careful just the same."

"I will. You ready to go downstairs for prayers?" Zohar asked.

"Let's wake Brother Jacob first."

After prayers and breakfast, Ben sat on a bench under a birch tree in the cloister. Blue birds were singing. He silently read from the Book of Psalms. Chapter 23, verse 3. *He restores my soul. He leads me in the paths of righteousness for His name's sake.* Ben paused to observe a monk pass with a bucket of hot soapy water; he set the bucket down and started scrubbing a life-size figure of Saint Francis, the patron saint of animals.

Ben closed his eyes and flashed back to the time he was a small boy. He was riding with his father on the horse-drawn wagon, delivering a Christmas tree in Beregszász. They stopped in front of a church, and little Ben watched the priest and his father pull a large fragrant evergreen off the wagon and haul it inside. Ben followed them, inhaling a sweet-smelling incense. The priest paid Ben's father and handed him a peppermint candy cane and gently patted his head. He fondly remembered then resumed reading Psalms, chapter 23, verse 5. *You prepare a table before me in the presence of my enemies. You anoint my head with oil; my cup overflows . . .*

Prior Mueller entered the cloister, and he walked over to where Ben was sitting.

"Good morning, Brother Benjamin."

"Good morning, Prior Mueller."

Ben made the sign of the cross, closed the Bible, and then looked up at the prior and smiled.

"Getting acquainted with your new surroundings, I see," the prior said as he noticed the gold-plated pocket watch on the bench.

"It's nice to sit out here," Ben said. "Peaceful."

"Yes, it is. What time is it?"

Ben reached into his robe pocket, forgetting that he had left the watch on the bench.

"There it is," the prior said, pointing.

"Oh . . . it's almost eight."

"That's a nice watch. Where'd you get it?" the prior inquired.

"Thanks. My father gave it to me."

"Can I see it?"

Ben handed him the watch, and the prior carefully examined it.

"It's old. Whoever made this did excellent workmanship. Does your father live in Hungary?"

The prior reluctantly handed Ben the watch.

"I don't know where my father is."

"And your mother? Does she live in Hungary?"

"*Nein,*" Ben answered in German.

"I'm sorry—I shouldn't be so meddlesome. If you're ready, brother, I'll show you where you'll be working today."

"Oh."

Ben grasped the handle on a small toolbox by his feet, and they left the cloister and headed toward the main annex of the abbey. The prior stopped when he felt a draft coming through the chapel doors. He closed them and turned to Ben.

"A few of the stained-glass windows are broken inside the chapel," he said. "They'll need to be replaced eventually. Gets too drafty. And the damn birds keep flying in and make an awful mess. I hate birds. Bothersome creatures. Wonder why God ever created them in the first place."

"How did the windows break?"

"Bombing from the American and British Air Forces," the prior snarled. "Shame the Luftwaffe can't blow them out of the sky more often."

"Oh . . . I should repair the windows before the winter sets in. Don't you think?"

"I'd have to ask the abbot first. Stained glass is expensive. And probably difficult, if not near impossible to find right now. You'll have plenty more windows to fix throughout the sisters' dormitory. We're going there now."

The two men climbed the stairs to the second floor. At the end of the hallway, a large open window let in an air that turned Ben's stomach. The prior coughed into his handkerchief.

"Smell that?" the prior inquired. "You should with that large nose of yours."

The prior chuckled behind his handkerchief.

"Oh—what is it?" Ben asked, stiffening his muscular shoulder blades.

"Smoke from the concentration camp down the road. Mauthausen. They burn dead bodies there."

"Oh, that's a terrible smell," Ben said, holding his breath and covering his nose and mouth with his hand.

"It is, indeed. That's how the Nazis get rid of the Jews who aren't working hard enough," the prior calmly stated.

"By burning them?"

"*Ja.*"

"Oh . . ."

"You say that often," the prior said. "Why is that?"

"Say what?"

"Oh."

"It's just a funny habit of mine."

"Habits can be broken, brother."

"Where are you from, Prior?"

"Nuremberg. Know where that is?"

"It's a city in Germany."

"You know your geography. Have you been there?"

"Never. I studied the countries of Europe while I was at the Archabbey of Pannonhalma."

"*Wunderbar.* Enough of the small talk," the prior said. "The sisters' rooms are on this floor." The two men stood in front of a door. "The brothers are seldom allowed up here, unless they have special permission from me or Abbot Zebedee. This is Sister Hildegard's room. Pardon her. She behaves a little strange sometimes."

"Oh?"

"She's the head baker at the monastery."

The prior knocked, and they waited several moments till a nun opened the door halfway. A young, brown-eyed woman smiled as she inquisitively looked at the men standing in the hallway. An abundance of wavy blond locks hung past her shoulders. She wore lipstick and a little makeup. Ben was awestruck by the sister's profound beauty.

"What is it, Prior?" she asked while momentarily gazing into Ben's hazel-green eyes. He felt something.

"Pardon the intrusion, Sister Hildegard. This is Brother

Benjamin. He's one of the three new monks who've come from Hungary."

"Welcome, brother," the sister greeted in Hungarian.

"Thank you. It's a pleasure to meet you, Sister Hildegard."

"Brother Benjamin will be repairing the broken windows at the monastery," the prior said. "He speaks German quite well. And a little English. If it's not too much of an inconvenience, he'll repair your window today."

"I'm delighted it's finally going to be fixed," she said. "Come in, brothers."

The men followed the nun inside, and she walked over to the only window in the room: a large, wood-framed window with four separate panes. Three of its panes were missing; weathered cardboard had been barricaded there instead.

The prior sneezed from the incense that burned from a hanging metal censer nearby. He looked critically at the sister's display of wavy blond hair, not approving of her rose-colored lipstick either.

"I believe it's time for a haircut, Sister Hildegard," the prior announced. "And what is that red stuff on your lips? —you know we don't approve of that here."

"I can manage my own affairs, thank you," she said, giving the judgmental prior a reproachful glance. She gathered her hair into a bun, attached a clip, and then yanked a hood over her head. She wiped her lips with a cloth. "That beard of yours could use a trim, prior," she said in a rather brusque manner.

His pale-skinned nose and cheeks flushed with embarrassment. He sniffled some. And sneezed again.

"I'll leave you to your work now, brother," the prior said. "If you need anything I'll be in Abbot Zebedee's office."

"Prior?"

"*Ja*, Sister?"

"Would you kindly burn some incense in the hall. It's beginning to smell like death out there. Leave the censer on the hook when you're done."

"*Ja*."

Ben opened the toolbox, took out a ruler, and measured the window frame. He took a pencil and jotted down the dimensions on a piece of scrap paper. In the meantime, Sister Hildegard removed her hood and released the hair clip, allowing her full head of sun-bleached locks to hang free again. She reapplied more rose-colored lipstick and puckered her lips. She looked at herself in the mirror.

"He can be quite a nuisance sometimes," she stated.

"Oh?"

"Prior Mueller."

The sister watched as Ben scraped the hardened putty and jagged bits of glass from the frame's edges.

"You can put that in here," she said, handing him a small cardboard box.

"Thanks."

After cleaning the window frame, Ben swept the mess into the box, and rested in front of the open window. He had worked up a sweat. Sister Hildegard handed him a glass of water.

"Thank you, Sister."

"You're welcome. There's that terrible odor again," she said, while pinching the end of her nose. "I'll have to burn more incense in here. I know you've only been at the monastery a short time, brother . . . but how are you finding Saint Clemens?"

"It's a very pleasant monastery. And the other brothers and sisters have been extremely helpful to us."

"You mean your two friends?"

"*Igen.* The prior told me that you're the head baker here."

"I am."

Ben started to say, "The bread here is far better than the ca—" He abruptly stopped himself.

"You mean the Archabbey of Pannonhalma?" the sister asked, looking at her face in the handheld mirror again. "Abbot Zebedee told me where you and the other two brothers have really come from."

"He did?"

"Mauthausen—don't fret, brother—I wouldn't tell a soul. Just remember what the abbot said regarding Prior Mueller. He can never be trusted."

"Of course."

The attractive sister moved closer to Ben.

"Do you like the color of my lipstick?" she inquired.

"I do. It's a pretty red."

"I'm not allowed to wear it outside the room. Abbot Zebedee doesn't mind, but the prior pitches a fit if I do."

Sister Hildegard moved closer and stood face to face with Ben now. They looked into each other's eyes. He smelled a pleasant fragrance of spices on her clothing. Ben felt a spark of electricity just as she came close enough to kiss him on the lips. She suddenly turned away and glanced toward the open window.

"There's that horrible smell again," she said.

"I'll go downstairs to the basement and cut some glass. I won't be long."

"When you return, brother, you don't have to knock. Just come in—I'll be expecting you."

"All right."

Downstairs by his workbench, Ben cut three measured pieces of glass, crumpled a page of old newspaper, and then cleaned the panes with a spritz of ammonia. The glass shone like new afterward. Pleased with his work, the glazier wrapped the glass in newspaper and turned off the light above his worktable. He left the basement and climbed the staircase to the third floor. He hastened down the hall, stopping in front of Sister Hildegard's door; he was about to knock when he remembered what she had told him before he left for the basement. Ben turned the black knob and pushed the door open. When he entered the room, a thick grayish-blue cloud of sweet-smelling frankincense enveloped him; it was almost overwhelming. Meanwhile, a purplish-violet light poured in through the broken window.

"I'm back, Sister Hildegard."

Ben heard the sister speak, but not from inside the room; her voice sounded as if it carried in on a breeze outside the window.

"Brother . . . I didn't think you'd be returning that fast."

"Is that you, Sister?"

"*Igen . . .*"

When the incense smoke dissipated, he saw that the sister was undressed; her backside faced him. A violet aura surrounded her nude, sunlit body. Ben was so transfixed, he was unable to speak, move, or breathe. He wanted to leave the room, but his shoes seemed as if they were well-glued to the floor. He trembled as an awesome fear came over him. He separated from his physical body, and his spirit rose. He touched the ceiling, and clearly saw that the sister's wavy blond hair dripped wet and hung all the way down her backside. Beads of moisture made her skin glow. Attached to her bare shoulder blades, Ben thought he saw what looked like a pair of glistening gold wings etched with white on their tips. He had never seen anything more terrifying yet beautiful in his entire life.

"Oh, my God!" he exclaimed, while the intense violet light bedazzled him.

"Don't be afraid, brother."

He felt a strong yet gentle pull. And his feet became planted inside his shoes again. The brother looked upon the sister's bare shoulders, but the gold wings were gone.

She spoke in a matter-of-fact tone. "I just came back from a shower. Step out of the room, brother. I'll only be a few minutes."

"*Igen.*"

Ben's feet weighed heavy; he moved one and then the other. He stuttered an apology and turned toward the door. He kept his balance in the hallway by holding his free hand against the wall. He felt dizzy. His mind reeled from what he had seen—what he thought he had seen. Not knowing whether to believe it or not, Ben pinched himself to see if he was dreaming.

A sister stopped when she noticed the monk awkwardly standing there, holding the glass wrapped in newspaper and bracing himself against the wall.

"Can I help you, brother? Are you lost?" she asked, snapping her thumb and forefinger.

"Who are you?" Ben asked the nun, as though he had just awakened from a deep sleep.

"Sister Saint Andrews. I'm the prioress at Saint Clemens."

"Oh."

"Monks aren't allowed on this floor. Are you all right, brother?"

"I felt a little dizzy before. I'm fine. It's from that awful smell."

"Yes, it's unusually bad today," the prioress stated.

Ben was still confused by what had transpired in Sister Hildegard's room.

"I don't believe I've ever seen you at the monastery until now," the nun said. "What's your name?"

Ben almost forgot. He remembered about the panes of glass that were tucked under his arm.

"I'm Brother . . . Brother Benjamin. I'm working up here, today."

"That's right. Abbot Zebedee mentioned it at breakfast. You're one of the new monks from Hungary. Welcome brother."

"Thank you."

"What kind of work do you do?"

"I fix broken windows."

"*Wunderbar*. Perhaps you could repair my window today. There's a terrible draft inside the room."

"I'd be happy to. As soon as I'm done with . . ."

"Brother Benjamin?" Sister Hildegard called from the threshold of her doorway nearby.

"*Igen?*"

"You can finish your work now."

19

Abbot Zebedee peered through his office window as a squadron of American B-17 bombers passed low over the monastery. Teacups, a sugar bowl, and spoons rattled atop a coffee table while picture frames shook against the wall.

"There they are again," the abbot mentioned as he caught site of the tail end of the flying fortress. "I hope it's the allies this time. Prior, why don't you heat up some more water in the kettle, please."

"*Jawohl,* commandant." The prior smirked, clicked his heels together, and gave a Nazi salute.

"That's not funny, Mueller. Not the least bit amusing."

Outside in the hall, Sister Hildegard held a plate of freshly baked blackberry scones; she stopped in front of the abbot's door and knocked.

"Come in."

"Morning, brothers," the sister greeted.

"Good morning, Sister Hildegarde," the abbot said, smelling the delectable-looking pastries on the plate.

"I have some blackberry scones—still warm from the oven—thought they'd go well with your tea this morning," the sister said, handing him the plate.

"Oh, they smell wonderful!" the abbot declared. "Thank you, sister. Joining us?"

"I would, but I have bread in the oven. Enjoy the scones."

The baker left, and the abbot chose a scone off the plate and inhaled the fresh-baked aroma. He took a bite. Then another.

"Would you care for one, Prior? They are delicious," the abbot asked, as his assistant turned off the gas flame under the tea kettle.

"No, thanks. I never liked the taste of blackberries."

"That's where we differ. Happens to be my favorite berry. Especially love them in pie. Yum. Nothing like a good blackberry pie."

"Try not to eat them all in one sitting," the prior said, pouring more steaming water into their cups.

"Please . . ."

"I find it strange those three new monks came here in the middle of a war," the prior stated. "Rather dangerous, in my opinion."

"Are you questioning the Lord's actions, Prior? Nothing is too dangerous as far as God is concerned. And I certainly have no qualms regarding the brothers. They're diligent workers, keep to the prayer schedule, and haven't caused us any problems so far."

"I suppose you're right."

"Suppose?"

"Brother Zohar looks like a good Christian man, but the other two monks seem different," the prior stated.

"How so?"

"Their noses are bigger than the average Gentile's nose."

The abbot laughed. He bit into a second scone.

"That's absurd, Prior. Big noses. Look at my nose. It's a large Roman nose but why would you think someone's facial features, or the size of their nose have anything to do with being a monk? There are several brothers and sisters at Saint Clemens who have long noses."

"That's true," the prior said. "It's completely irrelevant."

"Of course, it is—you're being utterly ridiculous."

"I'll be up in the library if you need me, Abbot. Afterwards, I have to run a few errands in town. The monastery is getting low on light bulbs, soap, and toilet paper. And Sister Hildegard requested some baking supplies. Can you think of anything else you need?"

"Chewing gum," the abbot replied. "Mint flavored. And a carton of cigarettes. Non-filtered, please. Here—you'll need some money—and don't forget to get the receipts."

Prior Mueller slowly climbed the vertiginous spiral staircase to the library. When he reached the top floor he approached the librarian's desk.

"Morning, Prior," the librarian softly spoke, glancing up from his book.

"Good morning, Brother Martin. When you get a chance, I want you to find the mailing address of Pannonhalma Archabbey. And the name of the abbot there. I believe it's located somewhere in Hungary."

"It is," the librarian spoke. "Happens to be the second oldest Benedictine monastery in the world. It was founded in the year 996. I once visited . . ."

The prior interrupted, "Thank you for the history lesson, Brother Martin, but all I need is the abbot's name and the mailing address of the monastery. I'll be at my table when you find it."

"Yes, Prior. I'll check on it now."

"*Gut.*"

The librarian leafed through the pages of a thick yellow book; he stopped at a section, scribbled a number, and then closed the book. He sharpened a pencil, then placed a phone call. The librarian conversed with someone and wrote something on an index card. He hung up the receiver and went over to where the prior was sitting.

"Here's what you requested."

"Good work, Prior. Come and have a glass of wine with me later this evening if you desire."

"I might just do that."

The librarian went about dusting and straightening a row of books while Prior Mueller read the information on the index card. He stroked his blonde bearded chin and thought for a couple of minutes, dreamily gazing out the library's picturesque window. A packed barge slowly drifted along the Danube below. He picked up his ink pen and composed a letter:

Dear Abbot Cooper,
Greetings from Saint Clemens Monastery. I hope everyone at Pannonhalma Archabbey is doing well through these most difficult times. Abbot Zebedee and I are grateful you sent us those three new brothers. They're well-behaved and hard-working monks. If there's anything I can do for you, don't hesitate to ask. God bless and enjoy the Benedictine and Brandy.

Sincerely Yours,
Prior Wilhelm Mueller
Saint Clemens Monastery

The prior left the library and descended the long spiral staircase. At the bottom he headed for the wine cellar. There, he chose a bottle then quickly went back upstairs to his office. He placed a bed of old newspaper into an empty cardboard box, gently placed the bottle of brandy and the envelope inside, and then taped it closed. He wrote FRAGILE GLASS, the return address, and the mailing address of Pannonhalma Archabbey on the front of the package. The prior left his office and drove the monastery's blue Mercedes to the post office in Melk, before running his other errands.

Two weeks later

A mail carrier stopped at the Archabbey of Pannonhalma, and an old monk signed for a package; he brought it down to Abbot Costello's office.

"You got mail, Abbot," the old monk announced, as he poked his funny-looking head and round stomach inside the doorway.

"Thank you, Brother Belluci. Leave it on the bench. And may God bless you always."

The old monk muttered a goodbye and returned to his little station near the front door.

While the warm sun rose higher on the horizon, Abbot Costello cut open the box and removed an envelope and a dark liquor bottle swaddled in newspaper. He read the label on it: Benedictine and Brandy. Made by monks at Saint Clemens Monastery. That's weird, he thought. The short and stocky abbot looked up and viewed the colorful Hungarian countryside through his office window. He reached for a brandy snifter on a shelf, then opened the bottle and poured himself a taste. He put down the glass, unsealed the envelope, and read the letter inside:

Dear Abbot Cooper,

Greetings from Saint Clemens Monastery. I hope you and your community at Pannonhalma Archabbey are doing well through these most difficult times. Abbot Zebedee and I are grateful you sent us those three new monks . . .

Abbot Costello finished reading the letter, and perplexedly scratched his head. *What three new monks is this Mueller character talking about?* Before the chubby little abbot of Pannonhalma sent Prior Mueller a telegram, he poured himself another drink and relaxed by the sunlit window in his office.

Back at Saint Clemens, Brother Benjamin swept and organized his work area before supper. He darkened the light over his worktable and hurried up the stairs to the dining hall. Brothers Jacob and Zohar had saved him a place at the monks' long, smoothly polished wood table. Abbot Zebedee and Prior Mueller sat across from the three brothers. The head baker and her assistants set baskets of heavenly smelling bread onto the brothers' and sisters' tables, while cooks carried in deep tureens of steaming-hot bean soup, platters of baked Danube salmon, and bottles of chilled white wine. Everyone bowed their heads and gave thanks.

Zohar nudged Ben's side with the pointy end of his elbow.

"The bread here is much better than those dreadful hard rolls they served us in the camp, hah, glazier? Pass the butter, please."

The prior suspiciously eyed the three Hungarian monks through the happy chatter in the dining hall.

"Careful what you say, Zohar," Ben whispered as the prior shot them another questioning glance.

"Sorry, I forgot," he said. "How's your work coming in the sisters' dormitory?"

"Fine," Ben replied. "Plenty of broken windows to repair. What about you?"

"I'm rigging up some lights on the outside of the monastery."

"How's that going?"

"Good."

Prior Mueller appeared annoyed as he picked a small bone out of his fish and showed it to the abbot.

"Look what I found."

"It's only a little bone."

"My fish seems a bit dry today," the prior said.

"Like your humor? Why can't we ever have a meal without you complaining about the food?"

The prior frowned as he placed the fish bone aside.

A monk approached the table and interrupted the two men.

"Excuse me, Prior. A telegram just came for you."

Prior Mueller put down his fork and knife and put on his reading glasses. He opened the telegram.

"Let's hear it, then," Abbot Zebedee said.

Dear Prior Mueller,

I'm overjoyed to hear that your three new monks are doing well at Saint Clemens, but I've only recently taken over the abbot's position here at Pannonhalma, and those three brothers you mentioned must have been sent while Abbot Cooper was still in charge of the monastery. I've never met the monks myself, and the brothers and sisters here have no recollection of them either.

Unfortunately, Abbot Cooper had some health issues and passed away shortly before I arrived. He would have been the go-to person with the most knowledge about this matter. The monks may have come from another monastery altogether. Perhaps you made a mistake. Regardless, stay safe, and May God bless you all at Saint Clemens. Fond regards to Abbot Zebedee, happy holidays, and thank you very much for the Benedictine and Brandy.

Sincerely yours,

Abbot Lou Costello
The Archabbey of Pannonhalma

Befuddled by what he had just read, Prior Mueller folded the telegram and rubbed his chin. "That's odd," he mentioned to Abbot Zebedee.

"What?"

"That Abbot Costello, or anyone else at Pannonhalma doesn't have any recollection of these three new brothers."

"Oh, well. It was thoughtful of you to send him a gift," Abbot Zebedee said. "I remember him well from the seminary in Rome. The pudgy little wise guy used to sit at the desk behind me. He loved to crack jokes and play tricks on me. All in good fun. Do me a big favor, Prior, and take my plate to the kitchen. If I'm needed, I'll be digesting my food out in the cloister. It's such a lovely day out."

"Yes, sir."

The large man stood and slowly departed the dining hall.

The prior silently read the telegram once more before placing it inside his robe pocket. He judiciously watched the three new monks rise from the supper table and bring their plates to be washed. The prior had another glass of white wine, as the late afternoon sunlight shone in through a dining room window.

Sister Hildegard hoisted a heavy sack of pastry flour onto her shoulder, and she left the dry goods storeroom in the basement. The baker was about to carry the sack up the basement steps when she bumped into Prior Mueller at the bottom of the staircase.

"Pardon me, sister."

"Prior . . . would you kindly take this flour to the bakery for me, please. I'm feeling a little weak today."

"*Ja*, of course."

The prior grunted as he lifted the thirty-five-kilo bag off the sister's shoulder and placed it onto his own.

"*Danke shoen*, Prior," Sister Hildegard said. "Use the wagon after you climb the stairs. I left it in the hallway. And leave the sack by the large mixer, please. God bless."

Prior Mueller was out of breath after climbing the flight of stairs. Someone had taken the wagon, so he had to carry the heavy load to the bakery. By then, he had forgotten all about his plans to interrogate the shoemaker. Completely exhausted, the prior retired to his room and had himself a lengthy nap before evening prayers.

Down in the basement, a strong leathery odor filled the musty air around the shoemaker's workbench. He was busy sewing a zipper onto a tall brown dress boot. Brother Jacob was so engrossed in his work; he was unaware that someone had been watching him a few moments.

"Those are lovely boots. I don't believe we've met. I'm Sister Hildegard. I work in the bakery."

The shoemaker glanced up suddenly.

"Sorry . . . I didn't mean to startle you."

"It's all right. I'm Brother Jacob."

The sister offered him a stick of chewing gum.

"Thank you."

"It's a pleasure to meet you, brother. I love the smell of leather. May I sit and watch you work?" she asked, brushing some flour off her apron.

"Be my guest."

"I met your friend, Brother Benjamin, the other day," she said. "He repaired the broken window in my room. I heard that you and your two friends are from Hungary."

"The Abbey of Archhalma. All three of us are from there," Brother Jacob stated.

The sister laughed.

"Is that funny?" Brother Jacob asked, testing the zipper on the boot.

"I'm sorry to laugh, brother . . . but I believe the monastery is called the Archabbey of Pannonhalma. You can speak Hungarian to me. I'm fluent in it."

"Are you Hungarian?"

"No, I'm an Austrian. I learned the language from some Hungarian sisters who once stayed at the monastery."

"How long have you been here?" he asked.

"Seems like forever sometimes. Who are you making the boots for?"

Brother Jacob went silent for a moment, then he spurted a reply: "Abbot Zebedee."

"Oh . . . how nice of you. My winter boots need new soles. Could you fix them?"

"I'd be happy to."

"There's no hurry. Winter won't be around for a few months." She warned in Hungarian, "Prior Mueller is suspicious of you and Brother Benjamin."

"I don't understand. What are you talking about?"

Brother Jacob put the boot aside and reached for the other one.

"Oh, I think you do, brother. The abbot told me everything about you and your two friends. You've all come from Hungary, but not from the Archabbey of Pannonhalma. You and Brother Benjamin once lived in Beregszász. Brother Zohar is from Budapest. The three of you recently came from the camp in Mauthausen."

"How do you know all this?" the shoemaker nervously inquired.

"As I said before, Abbot Zebedee told me. There's no reason to lie, brother. And the boots you're making are not for the abbot. I highly doubt he'd wear Nazi boots. Besides . . . if they were for him, they'd be too small for his feet. Those look like a size ten. The abbot wears a size thirteen."

"What else did the abbot tell you?"

"We spoke about Major Himmel—the man who brought you from the camp. I know the major and his wife. We come from the same place."

"You do?"

"There's no need to be frightened, brother. Your secrets are safe with me. I'll tell no one."

Brother Jacob held up the boot and inspected it.

"You do superb work."

"Thank you."

"I'm here to help you and your two friends keep safe from the Nazis. You must be careful, though. Prior Mueller has a friend at the camp. They talk sometimes. His name is Sergeant Heimlich."

"We've met," Brother Jacob stated. "Should I tell Brother Benjamin and Brother Zohar about this?"

"I already have. It's been nice chatting with you, brother. I'll bring you my boots tomorrow. Winter will be upon us before you know it."

20

Early autumn arrived at Saint Clemens and the oak, maple and birch leaves gradually faded to vibrant hues of cadmium orange, golden yellow, bright saffron, fiery red, burnt carmine, vermilion, primrose, livid pink, and finally dead-leaf brown. In the last days of October strong winds and heavy rains shook the brittle foliage off the branches, until all the trees and bushes stood naked around the monastery. (All except for the evergreens that is.) The weather turned cool and dry. For a week, the sisters and brothers raked the leaves into several large piles and burned them under the night skies. Sometimes, but not always, the fragrant, glowing red bonfires would completely cloak the odorous smoke that blew in from Mauthausen and its sub-camps.

By the beginning of November, the first frost had collected on the lawns and gardens at the abbey. Rabbit, fox, weasel, lynx, deer and wolf took refuge within the evergreen forest, preparing for the winter months by growing their warm furry coats and sweaters. The creatures pensively watched the landscape surrounding the monastery grow more barren. Little gray and brown field mice pitter-pattered outside the doors of Saint Clemens, hoping to gain access before the first snowfall.

On Ben's 25th birthday the third week of November, after breakfast, he, Brother Zohar, and Brother Jacob put on their winter coats and gathered out in the chilly cloister. They rested on a bench where Ben always sat, under a leafless birch tree. The late autumn sun weakly shone between the birch branches, alighting upon the saintly statues there. The blue birds that had once nested in the tree had flown south; they were replaced by two ominous-looking crows who sang a raspy operetta of caws, clicks, and shrieks. To chase the crows off, Brother Zohar stood like a tall scarecrow with his arms straight out. The lanky brother sat while the crows flew up to the roof and perched onto the two crosses there. The brothers listened while Ben finally divulged his secret. Of course, they were skeptical at first, when he told them what happened to him inside Sister Hildegard's room, the day he repaired her window. How he walked into the frankincense-filled room, the brilliant amethyst light inside, the way he left his physical body and viewed the sister from his spirit above. The men became excited when Ben spoke about Sister Hildegard standing naked by the broken window; how her broad, magnificent gold wings were etched with white on their fringes; the mystical way in which she revealed herself to him; and the divine nature of everything. The other two brothers believed him in the end.

Later that afternoon, after supper, Sister Hildegard surprised Brother Benjamin with a huge birthday cake she had baked and decorated with chocolate buttercream frosting. Abbot Zebedee, Prior Mueller, and all the brothers and sisters joyfully watched as Ben made a wish and blew out three candles on the cake. Everyone enjoyed a slice of cake, an extra glass of wine, and a healthy shot of Benedictine and Brandy. That evening a wind carried in a freeze from the alps, and the brothers and sisters fired up the potbelly stoves and hearths inside the abbey. Dark gray clouds formed above the abbey, and large wet snowflakes splattered onto Abbot Zebedee's windowsill outside his office. He dreamily watched the snow fall. The telephone rang. Commandant Graben greeted him on the other end. They talked for a few minutes. The abbot hung up the phone and quickly left the office and rushed to Prior Mueller's room down the hall. He knocked.

"Who is it?" the prior asked as he was just about to climb into bed.

"Abbot Zebedee."

"I'm going to sleep," the prior said behind the door. "Can it wait till tomorrow morning?"

"I'm afraid not."

The prior opened his door. "What is it, Abbot?"

"My apologies for disturbing you so late. Abbot Joseph at Melk Abbey asked me a big favor—he needs someone to help him organize his books for a few days—his prior fell sick; he's in bed with pneumonia. I told him you would do it. I'm giving you some money to give him, since we're financially stable right now."

"When will all this be taking place?"

"Tomorrow." The abbot handed the prior an envelope. "There's one thousand deutsche marks inside. Give it to Abbot Joseph when you arrive. Pack a bag now. You'll leave for Melk Abbey the first thing in the morning. A car will take you and bring you back. Sleep well, Prior. And God bless you for helping out."

"*Ja, gut nacht,* Abbot," the prior said in a coarse-grated German.

The abbot strode through the hall and walked his great body up the stairs to the monks' dormitory. He breathed heavily as he knocked on Brother Benjamin's door.

"Abbot Zebedee . . . what's the matter?"

"Something unexpected came up—we need to talk."

"Come in."

"I just got off the phone with the commandant at Mauthausen. He told me the Gestapo will visit the monastery two days from now."

"How would that concern me?" Ben asked.

"The commandant doesn't know that you and your two friends are here. If he finds out—we'll all be dead. I have to figure out a plan. It's cold in here," the abbot said, rubbing his large hands together.

"I'll build a fire."

Ben quickly crumpled up newspaper and put it inside the small wood-burning stove; he added kindling, struck a match, and the paper ignited. He added split logs before closing the door on the stove.

"Napoleon Bonaparte once stayed in this room," the abbot mentioned.

"Oh?"

"When the French occupied Austria. Napolean and his army traveled through this area. That's the rumor I heard anyway. I have a great idea, brother."

"What's that?" Ben asked while he opened the flue on the stove pipe, allowing the fire to cook hotter. In a few moments the room became toasty warm.

"That's much better," the abbot said.

"Please, have a seat, Abbot."

"*Danke.*"

Abbot Zebedee rested on the chair by the desk, crossing his brawny arms over his barrel chest. Ben sat on the bed and listened, while the abbot spoke to him in German.

21

Raphael removed a large cardboard box from the trunk of Major Himmel's blue Mercedes, and he leaned it against the car. The major buttoned his long wool coat and stepped from the car onto a thin layer of frozen snow. It crunched beneath his drab, well-worn military boots as he walked toward the monastery's entrance and read a notice on the door: *The doorbell is broken. Please use the doorknocker.* The sound of the knocker reverberated within the abbey's long, cold hallway. The noise awakened a snowy owl outside, who had taken up residence inside the eaves of the monastery's cupola. The white-feathered creature hooted once, closed its yellow eyes again, and then buried its black beak inside its warm chest feathers. The owl slept the entire day before its nightly hunt for dinner.

A monk opened the front door.

"Good morning, Major. How can I help you?"

"Good morning, Brother Zebulon. I have a delivery for Abbot Zebedee."

By coincidence the man of great stature happened to be close by, walking the abbey's Saint Bernard.

"Here he is now. He's just come back from his morning walk," the welcoming monk announced. "You have a visitor, Abbot."

"Major Himmel. What a pleasant surprise," the abbot said. "He's harmless."

The Saint Bernard approached the high-ranking officer, and it licked the major's glove-less hand. The officer patted the dog's big furry head.

"How are those three monks from Pannonhalma working out?" the major inquired.

"Excellent."

"I'm here to pick up the boots I ordered from the shoemaker—so, I thought I'd bring the monastery an early Christmas present."

The major pointed to the large rectangular box with a festive red ribbon and bow tied around it. FRAGILE GLASS had been written on the box.

"Oh, splendid," the abbot said.

"There are three stained-glass windows inside," the major announced. "To replace the broken ones in the chapel. It was quite drafty in there the last time my wife and I were here."

"That was very kind of you, Major." The abbot turned to a monk who was standing by the doorway. "Go tell Brother Benjamin to come to the front entrance immediately. Inform him that a delivery of glass has just arrived. And tell him to bring the handcart with him."

"Where might the glazier be?" the monk asked.

"I believe he's working in the infirmary," the abbot replied. "Just curious, Major. How did you know the size of the glass?"

"I measured one of the windows the last time I was here," the officer replied. "I'm pretty handy with a ruler, you know. Oh, by the way . . . do you happen to know where Brother Zohar is working today? I'd like to have a word with him after I collect my new boots."

"He's putting up Christmas lights in the dining room. Brother Zebulon, would you accompany the major through the abbey, please. And Major?"

"Ja?"

"After you finish your business, you and your driver should come by my office later. I'll have some sandwiches and coffee prepared before you get back on the road."

"Wunderbar."

Major Himmel and Brother Zebulon descended the staircase to the basement; they walked through a cool hallway and approached the shoemaker's workbench. His area was warmed by a small woodburning stove.

"Good morning, Brother Jacob," the major greeted.

"Ah, Major. It's nice to see you again. Your boots are ready. I was just putting a final polish on them."

"Oh . . . they look fabulous!" the major declared. "Don't they, Brother Zebulon?"

The elderly monk nodded his head in agreement. The major picked up a boot and felt the smooth leather. The mirror-like shine on the shoe enabled him to see his true reflection.

"Try them on," Brother Jacob said.

"Before I forget . . . here's my payment for the boots. It's five hundred deutsche marks. That
should be enough to cover the cost of your labor and materials."

"I can't accept that, Major. It's more money I would charge to make ten pairs of boots."

"Take it," the major said, handing the cobbler an envelope. "You'll need the money after you
leave the monastery."

"Danke schön, Major."

"Bitte schön."

Brother Jacob stashed the money in his robe pocket. The major sat on a chair, and the shoemaker helped him remove his old boots. The brother unzipped the new boots and the officer put his feet inside. Brother Jacob zipped them both up.

"Take a walk and see how they feel."

The major stood and walked around some.

Well . . . what do you think, Major?"

He looked at the shoemaker and smiled.

"Very comfortable. You did a wonderful job, Brother Jacob. I'll be sure to recommend you to my higher-ups."

"Wear them in good health, Major."

"Danke schön. You can burn the old boots," the major instructed.

He turned to Brother Zebulon, "Shall we see the electrician now?"

22

At seven o'clock in the morning, a pale sun broke through the haze over Mauthausen. A Kübelwagen and two military trucks exited the camp, and their tires turned a light cover of snow into slush along the slippery route. A zealous Sergeant Heimlich had detached a Nazi convoy that consisted of himself, Corporal Wagner, three German shepherds, and eight other gun-toting Gestapo. The convoy drove up a treacherously steep hill and slid into Saint Clemens's snow-covered parking lot. The warmly dressed militia got out of their vehicles and tiredly flapped their arms up and down and goose-stepped past the abbey's bell tower. Long pointed icicles had formed under the parapets above the entrance; one broke loose and dropped, barely missing the sergeant's head as he overanxiously used the doorknocker several times. Abbot Zebedee finally appeared.

"Good morning, Sergeant Heimlich. Haven't seen you in ages."

"*Ja . . . guten morgen,* Abbot. It's time you fixed your doorbell. *Hei?*"

"Our electrician will see to it soon, Sergeant. Come in, gentlemen. And please . . . wipe the snow off your boots. I have hot refreshments prepared for you in the dining hall. Right this way."

The Gestapo marched inside and slowly lumbered through the hall, passing a nervous group of hooded nuns who rapidly vanished down the marble-floored corridor. The militia was escorted into the dining hall and seated at a long table, where brothers and sisters served them a continental breakfast of coffee, tea, and warmed apple strudel.

"How's life back at Mauthausen, Sergeant?" Abbot Zebedee asked, while a sister poured steaming hot coffee into the Nazi's cup.

The sergeant gobbled down a bite of strudel and replied, "*Alles ist gut*. We are liquidating more and more Jews every day. In addition to any gentile political dissidents who are uncooperative with the Führer's cause."

"And . . . this is what your Führer calls the final solution?" the abbot inquired.

"That's correct," the sergeant replied, stuffing another pastry down his throat.

"May God have mercy on their souls," the abbot said, as he crossed himself.

The sergeant brushed some strudel crumbs off his army coat and gave the large clergyman a look of disapproval.

"You know, Abbot . . . talking in such a manner could be considered quite dangerous. It's forbidden to sympathize with the enemy. If you would like, I could easily arrange a private cell for you in Mauthausen."

The abbot remained sullen faced.

"Do you understand me, Abbot?"

"Yes, of course."

"*Gut*. Who made the apple strudel?" the sergeant asked while he reached for another pastry.

"A sister here bakes it."

"It's delicious. Could you get me the recipe?"

"Yes."

"*Wunderbar*. Commandant Graben would like more bottles of wine and brandy. All our supplies at the camp are waning. Winter has arrived early this year. We'll need blankets, socks, and whatever food provisions you can provide us."

"Don't worry, Sergeant. It'll all be prepared before you leave."

"And where are the brothers and sisters right now? It's quiet as a church mouse in here."

"You're in a monastery, Sergeant, don't forget. Many of the brothers and sisters are praying in the chapel. The rest are busy with their various chores throughout the abbey."

"I see."

The other men in the Gestapo made idle conversation while they chain-smoked bad-smelling cigarettes, polluting the atmosphere inside the dining hall. Abbot Zebedee asked a monk to open one of the windows there. A freezing fresh air blew in.

"And where's my good friend, Prior Mueller?" the blue-eyed sergeant asked the abbot.

"He took a few days leave at Melk Abbey."

"That's a shame. I was hoping to speak with him," the Nazi said. "Have you heard about the escape that occurred at the camp not long ago?"

"*Nein,* Sergeant. I haven't. We lead a fairly reclusive life at Saint Clemens. I wasn't aware of an escape."

"It was announced over the radio. I'm sure you must have a radio."

"We do. But I seldom have time to listen to current events," the abbot stated.

"You should. We're still looking for a handful of escaped prisoners who might have wandered through this area. Three Hungarian men in particular. You haven't seen them at the monastery by any chance?"

"*Nein.* I doubt anyone besides a monk, or a sister could survive this place for very long," the abbot replied. "What do these Hungarian men look like, Sergeant?"

"One has straight black hair, is young, tall, and skinny. Olive-colored complexion. He's a Christian man, and an electrician. Another man is a light-skinned Jew, in his early twenties. He's short, has brown hair, hazel green eyes, and muscular arms, back and shoulders. He has a birthmark on the side of one of his nostrils. He works with glass. The other escapee is a Jew also. Early forties I would say. He's short and scrawny looking. Light-skinned as well. He's a shoemaker."

"Do any of these Hungarian men wear eyeglasses by any chance?" the abbot questioned.

"*Nein.*"

"Sergeant. You and your men are welcome to look around—but I doubt it will be much use," the abbot said.

"Just the same, we'll require a complete search inside and outside the monastery. And while we're occupied with that, prepare the supplies I requested. And don't forget about that delicious Benedictine and Brandy you make here. *Achtung!* Wagner?"

"*Ja?*"

"Abbot Zebedee will accompany you to the kitchen and bakery now. Afterward, he'll take you up to the library. You three men search the chapel, the offices, the laundry, the basement, the catacombs, and outside around the building. Take two of the dogs with you. The other five men and I will check the brothers' and sisters' rooms. Let's go."

In the monastery's busy kitchen, Corporal Wagner saw double when he removed his coke-bottle eyeglasses and wiped the vapor off with a cloth; he returned them to his squinch-eyed face and watched the brothers and sisters chop vegetables and scale, clean, and bone fresh fish monks had caught in the Danube. Other nuns scrubbed surfaces from top to bottom, while the near-sighted Nazi inspected the immaculate kitchen. The corporal approached a stove where a short but able-bodied sister stood. Her hood concealed her forehead; she wore makeup and bifocal eyeglasses. The contents in the pot she was stirring gave off a steamy, pungent odor of onion, oregano, garlic and cabbage. The sister glanced up at the Nazi through her steamed-up spectacles. He sneezed.

"Something smells *wunderbar,*" the corporal said. "What's for supper, *fräulein?*"

The broad, able-bodied sister leaned over the pot and marinated its contents. She replied in a high-pitched German, "Stuffed cabbage. Heil Hellmenz, Corporal."

"Hungarian food. Smells delicious. Carry on with your work. And Heil Hellmenz, Sister."

"*Ja.*"

The strong nun by the stove covered the pot with a lid, and she bent down and whispered in the ear of a tall sister who was scrubbing the floor on her hands and knees. That sister also wore eyeglasses. "We're dead if they find the commandant's radio in your room," Brother Benjamin softly spoke.

"It's gone," Brother Zohar whispered back. "The major took it from me yesterday."

Two men from the Gestapo patiently waited in the monastery's dimly lit wine cellar while an elderly nun packed bottles of wine and liquor into boxes. She wore horn-rimmed glasses, makeup, and a pretty shade of lipstick Sister Hildegard lent her. The men carried the boxes out of the cellar, up the stairs, and on the back of one of the military trucks. One of them mentioned to the other while they took a cigarette break, "Manfred, did you see how ugly that sister looked down there?"

"*Ja.* My grandmother is prettier. C'mon—we have more boxes to load. This place gives me the creeps already."

"Her perfume smelled nice," the other man teased.

"*Schnell*, Werner."

Disguised in the nun's habit, Brother Jacob stood with a broom in a cool dark alcove of the wine cellar and warily watched the soldiers leave with the last two boxes of vino. He smiled and carried on sweeping the floor.

In the bakery, Sister Hildegard gathered up a large pile of bread dough from the mixer, and she kneaded it on a floured workbench. She looked up from her work when the abbot and the corporal entered the bakery. She nodded and gave the Nazi a teeth-clenched grin.

"This is one of our hard-working bakers, Sister Hildegard," the abbot introduced. "Corporal Wagner is here with the Gestapo, Sister. They are looking for some prisoners who've escaped from Mauthausen."

"Oh?"

The sister smiled and sprinkled some bread flour onto her worktable. "Be my guest," she said, forming the soft dough into a round clump and placing it onto a parchment-covered bake pan to proof. She took hold of another clump of dough and started working with that.

"By the way, Sister, do you happen to have the recipe for your apple strudel?" the abbot inquired. "Sergeant Heimlich would like to borrow it."

"It's in my drawer. I'll get it for you."

While the corporal slid his dirty fingernails along the baker's workbench, he sniffed the doughy air and stuck two of his fingers into a bowl of whipped cream. He licked his fingers then smiled. The abbot showed him through the rest of the bakeshop, and the two men turned to leave.

"I found the recipe, Abbot," the sister said, handing him an index card.

"Thank you. Have a blessed day," the abbot said while he winked at the sister.

"You as well, gentlemen."

After the men left, the baker dumped the bowl of whipped cream down the sink.

The abbot and the corporal proceeded through the hall, in the direction of the steep spiral staircase which led up to the monastery's library. They slowly ascended the staircase.

"Watch your step, Corporal," the abbot warned. "You're not afraid of heights, are you?"

"*Nein.*"

The Nazi nervously held the wrought-iron railing and glanced at the colorful frescoes painted high above his head. They finally reached the top step and entered a large room filled with sunlight.

"This is our library. Do you like to read, Corporal?"

"It's not one of my favorite pastimes."

The circular ascent had caused the soldier's focus to spin around and make his head swim momentarily.

"Are you all right, Capitan?" the abbot asked.

"*Ja*," the corporal replied, as he wiped the sweat from his brow, regained his equilibrium, and then followed the abbot through the library.

"This is our head librarian, Brother Martin," the abbot introduced. "Brother Martin, meet Corporal Wagner. He's from the camp at Mauthausen. I'll be giving him a tour of the library."

"Welcome, Corporal," the librarian spoke, as he made the sign of the cross, then returned his attention to the Book of Proverbs.

"This way," the abbot said. "Our library houses some of the oldest religious manuscripts in the world, but that wouldn't interest you much. Not being a reader."

"*Nein.*"

After the abbot and the corporal were finished, they approached the librarian's desk once more.

"Well, I hope that satisfies your curiosity, Corporal," Brother Martin said. "You can rest assured . . . we're not hiding any of your escaped prisoners up here."

"*Gut*," the corporal said, as he and the abbot left for the long staircase again.

"Watch your step," Abbot Zebedee said as he motioned for the poor-sighted soldier to go first.

After a few turns around the spiral stairs, the corporal stopped to clean his fogged-up glasses when they slipped from his hands. He tried to catch them, but he lost his balance and fell over the railing and plummeted to the bottom. A sister heard the corporal's neck crack when he hit the hard marble floor. Her loud shrieks echoed through the monastery. The librarian jumped off his stool and ran to the top of the staircase.

"Oh, Jesus! What happened?"

Shocked, the abbot looked over the railing. "Someone call the ambulance!" he hollered in vain.

Miraculously, the corporal's thick glass lenses remained intact when they landed on the floor. Several brothers and sisters gathered around the corporal while he convulsed some, then went still. The abbot reached the bottom of the staircase and hurriedly approached the group.

"Call the doctor," he ordered.

Feeling the corporal's pulse, a monk answered, "That won't be necessary; he's already gone."

"Oh, my God," the abbot said, as he bowed his head and made the sign of the cross.

Sergeant Heimlich and a few of the other Nazis came running after hearing the commotion.

"What happened to him?" the sergeant asked.

"He fell off the stairs," the abbot replied, pointing to the top of the staircase. "He was rushing and lost his balance—it was an accident."

"An accident?" the sergeant questioned, as he closed the corporal's eyes.

"Yes," the abbot explained, "he dropped his glasses and fell over the railing when he tried to catch them."

"Perhaps you accidentally pushed him, hah, Abbot?"

"Definitely not—he was too far ahead of me," Abbot Zebedee replied.

"Put him on the truck," the sergeant ordered two of the soldiers. "Are all our supplies packed?" he asked a monk in charge of the provisions.

"*Ja.*"

"Let's get out of here, then," the sergeant gruffly said. "And you're coming with us, Abbot."

"Why on earth for?"

"I believe the commandant will need to interrogate you about Corporal Wagner's death."

"But I had nothing to do with it," the abbot pleaded.

"Then you'll explain that to the commandant," Sergent

Heimlich said. "Along with how sympathetic you feel about the Jews."

"I'll need to get my coat first."

"Hurry, then . . ."

The next day, Prior Mueller returned to Saint Clemens and found that Abbot Zebedee was absent from his post. He read a note taped to the abbot's desk, informing him about the mishap which took place at the monastery, and that the abbot had been taken to the concentration camp for interrogation. The message had been signed by Prioress Sister Saint Andrews. The prior picked up the telephone and nervously dialed the camp. A switchboard operator answered:

"Mauthausen . . . can I help you?"

"Hello. Could you please connect me with the commandant?" the prior asked.

"Just a moment."

While the prior waited to be connected, he noticed a pair of coke-bottle eyeglasses on Abbot Zebedee's desk. He looked out the window at the wind-swirling snow. A white-tailed rabbit ran past.

"Commandant Graben speaking."

"Hello, Commandant. This is Prior Mueller from Saint Clemens Monastery."

"Hello, Prior. I was expecting a call from you."

"When will Abbot Zebedee be returning to Saint Clemens?"

"I have some good news and bad news for you, Prior. Unfortunately, because of the terrible incident that happened at the monastery, the abbot won't be coming back any time soon."

"Why is that?"

"From the information we gathered during our interrogation with Abbot Zebedee, a tribunal charged him with one count of manslaughter and several counts of verbally sympathizing with the enemy. It's very unfortunate but he was sentenced to ten years imprisonment with hard labor. The good news is, you'll be taking over the abbot's position immediately. Have a nice day, Abbot Mueller."

23

Christmas Day 1944

After everyone at the monastery ate their Christmas dinner of Weiner Schnitzel, yams, peas, and Linzer Torte, Abbot Mueller and Brother Martin celebrated the rest of the holiday by breaking into the last two bottles of Abbot Zebedee's private stock of Chianti. The two men became increasingly intoxicated while they listened to a BBC broadcast of the latest developments of World War II:

"On Christmas day, the American Third Army, under the leadership of General George Patton, the Second US Armored Division, halted enemy tanks short of the Meuse River," the radio announcer spoke.

"Sounds like the Germans may be retreating," the librarian said while Abbot Mueller poured more red wine into their glasses.

"Shame," the abbot said.

By the 16th of January 1945, the German army would ultimately lose the Battle of the Bulge, which was fought in the Ardennes Forest of Belgium and Luxembourg. On January 27, 1945, Soviet troops liberated the Auschwitz concentration camp, marking the beginning of the end of the Holocaust.

In the dead of winter, Ben put on his wool coat and went

outside to the woodshed. A diamond night sky sparkled above. An icy air embraced his neck. He shivered and covered his head with the hood. The mercury was below zero. Ben grasped a long-handled ax and proceeded to split a pile of birch and maple logs. After twenty minutes of hard physical exertion, he leaned the ax inside the woodshed and loaded the split wood into a wheelbarrow. He wiped his forehead, and steered the wheelbarrow through a back entrance, carting the wood inside the chapel. He removed his coat and scarf and stacked the split wood beside a hearth. Ben fed the fire, rested on a pew, and admired the three stained-glass windows he had installed before Christmas. The blazing orange flames magically reflected in the colored glass.

April 1945

At his work area in the basement Brother Benjamin heard large thawing sheets of ice and snow slide off the monastery's roof and crash to the ground. The snowy owl who had wintered on the cupola was awakened by the noise, and it flew off toward some tall spruce trees. The wide-winged owl never returned to its winter home.

Ben was depressed Abbot Zebedee was no longer at Saint Clemens. He placed a broom and dustpan aside, put on his coat, and then took a long walk around the grounds. He rubbed the sun's heat into his arms and breathed the fresh country air; it was exhilarating. He moved at a slightly faster pace. The ice on the Danube had melted, and the welcome sunlight gave life to the tiny greenish buds on the trees and bushes. *The leaves will appear again soon,* Ben thought. Before continuing his hike, he stopped to watch a long black barge along the river; he recognized the ship's white granite cargo.

By the end of April, Brother Benjamin spent more time outdoors. He had repaired most of the broken windows in the abbey, so he assisted some of the other brothers and sisters till the gardens and prepare the soil for the first planting of vegetable seedlings which were started in the monastery's greenhouse. He thought about his mother and father. He missed them.

In the basement, Brother Jacob continued to work on the sisters' and brothers' boots and shoes. He often ruminated about his wife, sometimes shedding tears over the happier times they had spent in Beregszász.

Brother Zohar occupied himself with his electrical duties throughout the abbey. He finally addressed the broken doorbell at the monastery's front entrance. He installed a new bell and tested it by pressing his lanky finger on the round button. It worked. He rang the bell a couple more times before an irate Abbot Mueller appeared in the vestibule.

"Brother Zohar. What's the matter with that damn bell? I thought you fixed it."

Zohar gave the abbot a broad smile. "I have. It's working now," the electrician happily replied.

"I heard! Now take down those Christmas lights around the monastery. It's almost May."

Brother Zohar tapped his heels together and raised his arm in a German military salute. *"Jawohl, Capitan."*

When May arrived, Sister Hildegard would finish her early morning tasks in the bakery and go outside to help Sister Saint Andrews plant tulip bulbs in the garden facing the abbot's office window. They would laugh the whole time as the baker's long blond hair flew in the blustery wind. Her lips were usually painted a pomegranate red. Abbot Mueller would scornfully observe the two women from his window.

Three weeks went by, and the flower bulbs the two sisters had planted, vigorously sprouted. A length of time afterward, several crimson, white, yellow and pink tulips appeared. Sister Hildegard and Sister Saint Andrews would happily cut and place the flowers into wicker baskets, bring them inside, and arrange the colored tulips in vases on the tables in the dining hall.

On one particular afternoon, Sister Hildegarde cut a basketful of tulips, left the garden, and carried the basket through the hallway of the abbey. She stopped to rest near the abbot's office, and, by coincidence, she clearly heard him having a conversation on the telephone.

"Sergeant, I believe there's something rotten in Denmark at the monastery," Abbot Mueller announced.

"What do you mean?"

"Haven't you heard that expression before?" the abbot asked.

"Of course, I have. Get to the fucking point, Mueller."

"A sister who works in the laundry found something inside the pocket of a monk's robe."

"What is it?"

"A faded yellow document of some sort," the abbot replied. "It looks official. I have it in front of me right now."

"Oh?"

Sister Hildegard heard every word the sergeant had said from the speaker on the desk phone.

"It's been washed out several times," the abbot stated. "Let me look at it with a magnifying glass. Ah, that's a little clearer, but the writing is too faded. There appears to be a signature. And some kind of symbol. I can't decipher it."

"The commandant needs more wine," the sergeant said. "I'll be at the monastery in the morning to look at it. *Gut nacht,* Abbot."

"I look forward to seeing you. *Gut nacht,* Sergeant."

Abbot Mueller hung up the phone and set the faded yellow document aside. He hardly noticed Sister Hildegard's shadow swiftly pass his open doorway. She hastened toward the dining hall and placed the basket of flowers onto a table.

24

Sister Hildegard unexpectedly appeared at Ben's worktable while he steadily guided his glass cutter along a windowpane. She startled him, and he misdirected the line of the glass cutter, leaving the pane unusable. He discarded the glass waste into a metal barrel.

"Sister Hildegard—I'm surprised to see you here this hour—thought you'd be getting ready for supper."

"Greetings, Brother Benjamin. You and your two friends must leave the monastery tonight."

"Why?"

"We can't talk here—come with me—we'll go out to the cloister," the sister said.

Ben darkened the light above his table, and they went outside and walked to a far end of the quadrangle, where a full moon's dazzling pearl-white shine caused a group of stone saints there to look alive. The sister peeked from behind a statue, taking care nobody else was around to listen.

"You and the other two brothers are no longer safe here," she said. "I overheard Abbot Mueller talk on the phone with his friend from Mauthausen. Sergeant Heimlich. He said a sister who works in the laundry found a suspicious-looking document in the pocket of a monk's robe. It may have come from the concentration camp. Mueller got hold of it—and informed the sergeant. One of you must have accidentally placed it in the robe when you changed clothes. The Gestapo are coming here early tomorrow morning. You'll have to leave tonight."

"How?"

"I'll steal the keys to the monastery's car and drive you across the border into Switzerland. Once you get there—you'll be out of harm's way."

"None of us have passports," the monk said.

"You don't need them. You'll apply for political asylum at the border."

"What about Abbot Mueller? I would think he'd be suspicious of the slightest activity around here."

"I'll take care of him," the sister said. "Tell the other brothers to prepare to leave tonight. And don't speak about this at the supper table. I don't want you to draw any unnecessary attention. Someone's coming—quick—we'll leave through the garden."

Sister Hildegard rushed to the apothecary's office, picked the door lock, went inside and opened a medicine cabinet. Using a flashlight, she discovered a bottle of sleeping pills and quickly left. The sister flew down the hall to the bakery where she removed a gold heart locket from around her neck and pulled a latch to open the little locket door. She ground the white pills in a mortar and pestle and filled the locket with the powdered sedative.

Abbot Mueller had entered the dining hall and noticed the neglected basket of tulips. He questioned a youthful sister who was setting a dinner table.

"Sister Mary?"

"Yes, Abbot?"

"What are these damn flowers doing here?"

"I don't know."

"Get them in water before supper starts."

"Yes, Abbot, I'll do it right away," Sister Mary answered.

"And fetch me a bottle of red wine. A cabernet, preferably."

"Yes, sir."

The young sister brought the basket of tulips to the kitchen. She selected a bottle of cabernet from a wine rack.

"I'll get the abbot his wine, Sister Mary," Sister Hildegard said. "You attend to the flowers. Please."

"Yes, Sister."

Sister Mary placed the tulips into six vases and added water from the sink. She brought the vases to the dining hall and set them on the two long tables.

"Where's that bottle of wine?" the abbot inquired from his seat.

"Sister Hildegard is seeing to it," Sister Mary replied.

"*Gut,*" the abbot said while ogling the young nun's softly curved figure.

Meanwhile, Sister Hildegard carried the wine bottle to the back storeroom and opened it with a corkscrew. She discreetly added the white powder from her heart locket, reinserted the cork, shook the bottle, and then delivered it to Abbot Mueller. She pulled out the cork and poured him a glass. He smiled and thanked her.

Monks and nuns carried baskets of bread and butter out to the dining hall, while the kitchen staff brought out supper. Soon afterward, the dining hall had filled with brothers and sisters. The monks sat and held hands at their long table; the sisters held hands at theirs. They said grace before helping themselves to steaming-hot stuffed cabbage. Ben's mother's recipe.

When Abbot Mueller was almost through with supper, he noticed the sisters' and brothers' faces had become animated and distorted. He finished drinking his second glass of wine, and everyone's voice sounded weird and garbled. The abbot started laughing for no reason. The drug inside the wine had taken effect. He swirled around the alcohol, spilling some onto the skirt of his robe. He inhaled the fruity bouquet while briefly noticing a powdery white substance on the surface. He guzzled the wine, then poured himself another glass. With his senses greatly impaired, the abbot loudly called to the young sister whom he had spoken to earlier. She was sweeping the floor nearby.

"Sister Mary."

"Yes, Abbot?"

"Come over here, please."

She stopped sweeping and approached him.

"Do you need something, Abbot?"

"*Ja.*" He suddenly grabbed the sister's wrist, twirling her around and slapping her behind. "What room number are you in, Sister? I'd like to have sex with you tonight."

"Abbot . . . please!" Sister Mary declared, as she pulled herself away from him and left.

The abbot laughed boisterously and banged his fists on the table. His drunken face twisted. The room spun in a wobbly circle as the brothers and sisters filed out of the dining hall, all except for Sister Hildegard and Brothers Ben, Jacob, and Zohar.

The abbot broke his wine glass on the floor.

"It's time for bed, Abbot," Sister Hildegard told him. "Let's take him to his room."

The three brothers helped the abbot stand, and they assisted him back to his room on the first floor. They stood in front of his locked door.

"Quick—someone reach into his pocket and grab his keys," the sister instructed.

Ben fished out the keys and gave them to the sister. She unlocked the door, and they put the sedated man to bed. Brother Jacob removed the abbot's shoes while Ben gently set his head on a pillow. Sister Hildegard covered the snoring abbot with a blanket. And Zohar darkened the light.

25

In Abbot Mueller's office, Sister Hildegard found the keys were missing to the monastery's blue Benz.

"He usually hangs them on this hook—Brother Ben—check the desk."

While Ben rustled through a drawer, he completely overlooked his former work pass at the camp. Zohar moved a bottle of Benedictine and Brandy that sat on a shelf; behind the bottle was a set of car keys. He dangled them in the air and asked, "Is this what we're looking for?"

"Yes," the sister said, and the lanky man tossed them to her. "Let's go, brothers—."

They bolted down the hallway and out the front entrance. The brothers followed the sister to the abbey's Mercedes. Ben sat in the front passenger seat while the other two brothers got in the back. The sister nervously placed the keys into the ignition. The engine wouldn't start at first. She pumped the gas pedal and turned the key again. That time it worked. She revved the engine. Soon after, hard pellets of rain hit the windshield. It thundered, and lightning struck the crosses on the monastery roof. The sister turned the wipers on high while Sister Saint Andrews pulled aside a curtain from a second-floor window; she watched Sister Hildegard put the car in drive and tear out of the parking lot. She rode down the steep drive, sped past the village of Melk, and headed toward the Autobahn.

After they had traveled a few kilometers, Ben broke the silence: "How far is to Switzerland?"

"About five hours. I pray we have enough petrol to make it there," the sister replied.

"How much do we have?" Zohar inquired.

"Almost a full tank."

Just then, a German military vehicle passed the Mercedes from the opposite direction; its swastika flags rapidly flapped on the outside of the vehicle.

"Oh, Christ!" Sister Hildegard exclaimed.

Brother Jacob peered through the rear windshield.

"Gestapo?" he asked.

"I'm afraid so," the sister replied. "They're probably on their way up to the monastery. Hold on, brothers; the road's a little dangerous through here."

The sister peeled around a tight curve; her high beams startled two wild boars who were digging tubers on the roadside; the bristle-haired animals scampered into the woods. The sister pulled onto the Autobahn, pressed her foot on the gas pedal, and drove at a high rate of speed.

The driver of the German military vehicle slammed on the brakes when he arrived at Saint Clemens. Sergeant Heimlich and two other Nazis hammered their heels up to the front door. The sergeant impatiently rang the doorbell until an elderly monk's face appeared from a small window-like opening on the door.

"A blessed night, isn't it, Sergeant?" Brother Zebulon greeted. "We needed the rain."

"Fuck you! Where is Abbot Mueller?"

"He's fast asleep. It's late," the monk replied.

"Let us in. I have reason to believe some escaped prisoners from Mauthausen are hiding at the abbey."

"Oh, Lord Jesus," the monk said. He closed the small window, unlocked the door, and opened it for the Gestapo. They barged in, and almost knocked the short monk to the floor.

"Where's the abbot's room?" the sergeant asked, as he tugged on the sleeve of Brother Zebulon's robe.

"This way."

They walked down the hall, and the monk stopped by a door and pointed his trembling finger. "That's his room."

The Nazis went inside and found the abbot dead asleep.

"Mueller, wake up!" the sergeant yelled.

He didn't stir. The sergeant picked up a wash basin of cold water and threw it onto the abbot's face. His nailed-shut eyes popped open and dilated.

"What in God's name is going on here?" the abbot inquired. "Sergeant—you're early—I thought you were coming in the morning."

"Get your ass up, Mueller."

"It feels like I've been drugged with something," the abbot said, while he wrenched himself out of bed and put on his shoes. He put his hands into his robe pockets. "My keys are missing. I probably left them in my office."

"Move," the sergeant ordered.

They briskly marched down the hall and found the abbot's keys in the lock of the open door. The lights were burning within. The desk was left in a disarray.

"Mother of God! Someone's been in here," the abbot exclaimed while noticing the disturbed condition of his office.

Just then, Sister Saint Andrews appeared in the open doorway with Brother Zebulon.

"Abbot—I saw Sister Hildegard drive away in the monastery car," she announced. "What in heaven's name are these soldiers doing here this hour?"

"When was that?" the sergeant asked the prioress.

"About forty minutes ago. I overheard her say she was going to drive the three brothers to the border in Zurich."

"What!" the abbot shouted.

"That must have been the blue Mercedes we passed on the way here," one of the other Nazis mentioned.

"*Ja . . .*"

Abbot Mueller opened his desk drawer and removed the

washed-out yellow document. "This is what I was telling you about on the telephone," he said as he handed it to the sergeant.

Sergeant Heimlich barely recognized the stamped seal of Mauthausen, a black eagle and swastika; his slap-dash signature; and Ben's printed last name, Weiss, somewhat legible.

"Weiss?" the sergeant said. "That's one of our work passes we use at the camp. You have a monk at the monastery who knows how to cut glass?" the sergeant inquired.

"*Ja*. . . a short, muscular-looking fellow. Brother Benjamin is his name. Why?"

"Brother? He's a Jew!" the sergeant screamed. "This was his work pass at Mauthausen. He escaped. With a shoemaker and an electrician. Have they been here also?"

"For several months now," the sandy-eyed abbot replied. "Abbot Zebedee told me the three brothers came from a monastery in Hungary. The Archabbey of Pannonhalma."

"He lied," the sergeant stated. "He was protecting the prisoners."

"I knew something was fishy from the start," the abbot stated.

"Let's get out of here and find that blue Mercedes. There's only one road to Zurich from here," Sergeant Heimlich told the other two Gestapo.

26

A family of deer meandered across the Autobahn, and they approached the shelter of their woodland home. Taking up the rear of the herd, the mother, a speckle-tailed doe, innocently clip-clopped to the middle of the highway, where she kicked over a small wooden box; the mother deer froze, heard a distinctive clicking noise, and then pensively watched her family as they safely entered the dark forest. Moments later the speckle-tailed doe moved its hoof slightly, and a landmine exploded. It scattered chunks of asphalt and smoke high above the road. The blast threw the doe off her feet, and she landed on the roadside. Her hind leg was severed, while its other back limb dangled from bleeding tendons and fascia.

Sister Hildegard and the three brothers had heard the explosion, nearing the scene of the accident. The sister swerved around a crater the bomb made in the road. She stopped on the shoulder. From the car's headlights and the burning brush, they observed the injured animal as its life-fluid rapidly escaped its arteries.

"My God!" the sister declared. "Please help that poor creature. Hurry, Ben, open the glove compartment and give me the pistol—be careful—it's loaded."

"Here . . . what do you need that for?"

"I have to put the animal out of its misery."

"Oh."

The sister and the three men got out of the car and approached the snorting animal. It breathed heavily. The other deer in the clan had stopped soon after the explosion; by instinct, the herd sensed that a member of their clan, their mother, had fallen behind. The animals in the forest turned toward the road and listened, while Sister Hildegard knelt and tried to comfort the injured doe. The three brothers watched as the sister gently stroked the soft gray fur on its neck. The doe calmed a little, looking at everyone with her coffee-brown eyes. The sister's bright gold angel's wings appeared, and she spread them over the animal. The three brothers felt a powerful sensation in the air.

"What happened to me?" the speckle-tailed doe grunted.

"You must have stepped on a landmine, my lovely creature," the angel replied. "It was an accident."

"My pain is excruciating."

"I know. Fear not . . . you'll be with the Almighty soon."

The animal glanced above. "Your wings are beautiful. Are you an eagle?"

"No . . . I'm an angel. I've come to help you return home."

The brothers were awestruck, as they watched the mother deer shed tears. In the forest her family cried also.

"Is there a way this can be made better?" the speckle-tailed doe beseeched the angel.

"Yes, there is . . ."

Sister Hildegard made the sign of the cross, released the safety on the pistol, and placed the barrel against the doe's wavering but still beating heart. She pulled the trigger.

"Let's go, brothers . . ."

A couple hours later, the sister drove into a tunnel while a train rolled by on the rails above. Inside the tunnel the sound of a German police siren was heard farther behind. The Mercedes Benz emerged from the tunnel. And a hint of daylight appeared.

"There's a sign up ahead," Zohar said. "It's two kilometers to Zurich."

"We're on empty," the sister said. "We won't make it."

Ben tuned in an English-speaking station on the radio. A

newscaster announced, "This is the latest news bulletin from the BBC in London. Today, the 8th of May 1945, Germany has officially surrendered. I repeat. German forces have surrendered. The war is over in Europe."

"Oh, thank God!" Sister Hildegard declared.

Everyone was overjoyed while light came over the trees. They watched a buzz of military vehicles pass them from the opposite direction. Soldiers happily waved to them. British, American, French, and Canadian flags triumphantly flew from their vehicles.

While the Mercedes drew nearer to the Swiss border, a German police siren blared from behind. Sister Hildegard glanced in the rearview mirror, and she saw a flashing red light from a Gestapo vehicle.

"We have them now," Sergeant Heimlich boasted while he confidently gripped his Luger pistol.

A patch of heavy fog suddenly descended upon the road, enveloping the two vehicles for a few moments. When the Kübelwagen came out of the fog, they saw that the monastery's blue Mercedes was idling on the shoulder of the highway. The morning's rays now shined magnificently upon the car hood. The Kübelwagen braked behind them. Sergeant Heimlich and the other soldiers got out; they drew their weapons and surrounded the car. Someone rolled down the window on the passenger side of the Mercedes, and the sergeant stared in disbelief.

"Major Himmel! —What on earth are you doing here?"

"Hello, Sergeant."

"Heil Hellmenz, Major," the sergeant said, saluting with his arm high in the air. "We'll relieve you of the prisoners now, Major."

"I think you made a big mistake, Sergeant," the major said. "And please . . . lower your arm. Your armpit stinks."

"Where are the three prisoners, Major?" the sergeant inquired, peering through the car's tinted back window.

"Are you out of your mind? —We have no prisoners with us."

A window opened, and Lieutenant Flügel and Captain Segan happily waved from the back seat.

"Lower your guns, gentlemen," Lieutenant Flügel ordered. "The war is over, Sergeant. Germany surrendered less than twenty minutes ago. You must have heard the news on the radio?"

"*Nein,*" the sergeant replied with an extremely puzzled look. The Gestapo holstered their pistols.

"Now, if you don't mind, gentlemen . . . we'll be continuing our journey into Switzerland," the major said. "We're meeting our wives at a lovely resort high in the Alps. Drive, Raphael."

"*Ja*, Major."

The high-ranking officers smiled, rolled up their windows, and Raphael drove the gleaming blue Mercedes into the golden dawn.

Still attired in their black monastery robes, Ben, Zohar, and Mr. Katz sat inside a room at a border station in Zurich. A Swiss woman dressed in a khaki uniform came out and served them egg sandwiches and coffee. They heard a train whistle blow not far-off.

"Now that the war is over—what are we going to do next?" Mr. Katz asked.

"Oh. You have money," Ben answered. "I suppose we could buy train tickets and return home to Beregszász."

"*Igen.* Maybe some of our friends and family will be there," Mr. Katz said. "And Zohar can go home to Budapest. And see his."

Tears fell from the lanky man's eyes.

"I have no friends or family left in Budapest. My mother and father died when I was a child. And I have no sisters or brothers. Nor aunts, uncles, or cousins that I know of. Perhaps, I could come with you guys?"

Ben consoled Zohar by placing a hand on his bone-thin shoulder.

"Of course, you can come with us, brother. We are your family now."

"Thank you, Ben."

"We can build a new life for ourselves," Mr. Katz said. "If not in Beregszász then somewhere else."

"Perhaps America," Zohar mentioned, beaming a broad smile now. "I heard that the streets are paved with gold there."

"*Igen*," Ben said as he opened his pocket watch. Eight on the dot. He stood and felt the glass cutter he had in his robe pocket. "How 'bout we find that train station now, brothers."

Glossary

achtung: attention! in German

Arbeit macht frei: German for, work will set you free. The ironic motto that was displayed on the entrance gate to the Auschwitz concentration camp.

ailes d'ange: French for 'Angel wings'

bimah: Hebrew for the podium, or platform where the ark in a synagogue is situated. Prayer services are led there, and the torah is read from.

bissel: a little or small amount. Yiddish

challah: a traditional braided bread baked for the Jewish Sabbath and holidays.

Chasid: a man of a strictly orthodox Jewish sect. Yiddish.

danke schön: German, for thank you very much

Die Endlösung der Judenfrage: German meaning, "the final solution"

fater: Yiddish for father

fräulein: unmarried young German woman

Haftorah: one of the biblical selections from the Books of Prophets, read after the torah is read in the synagogue during the Saturday morning service.

igen: Hungarian for the word, yes

Juden: German for Jews, singular, Jude

kinder: German for children

kübelwagen: A German light military vehicle used during WW2; it was the forerunner of the Volkswagen Beetle.

l'chaim: Yiddish interjection used in toasts, meaning "to life!"

jawohl: German for the word yes

mazel tov: Yiddish word meaning 'good luck' or congratulations meshugana: Yiddish slang for someone who acts in an insane manner.

mezuzah: a piece of parchment called a klaf, which is contained in a decorative case and inscribed with specific Hebrew verses from the Torah. These verses consist of the Jewish prayer, Shema Yisrael, beginning with the phrase: "Hear, O Israel, the Lord our God, the Lord is One."

muter: Yiddish for mother

nein: German word for No

roux: is a French term for a mixture of fat (especially butter) and flour used in making sauces.

shul: A Yiddish word referring to a synagogue. Comes from the German schule, meaning school.

schnell: quick, in German

schlep: Yiddish for 'to carry a cumbersome load'

schmutzig: German, for dirty or filthy

schweinehund: A German insult defined as, pigdog

tateleh: Yiddish, for an obedient little boy

tallis/tallit: a prayer shawl worn by Jews in the synagogue

tefillin, or phylacteries: A set of small black leather boxes and straps that contain scrolls of parchment inscribed with verses from the Torah. The tefillin are worn by observant Jewish men during weekday morning prayers said at home or in the synagogue

wunderbar: German, for wonderful

yarmulke: a head covering worn by observant Jews. Also known as a skullcap or kippah.

zie gesunt: Yiddish for 'be healthy'

Acknowledgements

Special thanks to my editor, Liz Ferry. Much appreciation and thanks go out to Professor Winston Aarons, my former writing teacher, who taught me a lot about fiction from his writing classes at the Old School Square in Delray Beach FL. Thanks to Dimitri, Sheri, Barbara, Petra and Kathy for your generous help with grammar, story and plot development. And most importantly—your patience, love, wisdom and laughter.

Do not fear the terrors of the night
nor the arrows that fly in the day.
Dread not the thief who lurks in darkness
nor the catastrophe that strikes at midday.
Although a thousand may fall at your side
and ten thousand perish around you,
these atrocities can't harm you.
See how the wicked are chastised.
If you make the Lord your home and refuge,
no bad influences will overpower you.
Just realize that the wicked are punished.
No disease will affect you.
For He will order his protecting angels,
everywhere you travel.

Psalms 91 verses 5-11

Other titles by the author
If Frogs Could Fly
'a psychedelic romp with a sixties undercurrent strangely
relevant to our times'
written under the pseudonym
E.B. Mendel

The author would love to hear what readers thought about the books. He can be contacted at sunbridgebooks@gmail.com